*WHIZZAP!* A blast from the fighter ship hit a manned guard tower. *KA-BOOM!* The tower exploded. The guards were disintegrated.

"Th-They have the totem! Turok, quick! Do something!" someone shouted.

"There's no way to disable the mother ship!" Turok cried as an idea occurred to him. "If only I could get to the top of the ship." Turok reached into his back pocket and affixed the Folding Eye device over his right eye. He spied several strange floating holes of varying sizes in the atmosphere. He dove headfirst into the first open portal.

*WHUMP!* Turok crash-landed on the top of the hovering spacecraft. "Now the party can begin," he announced. He got to his feet and aimed the plasma rifle at the hull of the mother ship.

*BLAM! BLAM! BLAM!* Powerful tracer rounds of plasma energy ripped through the metal, tearing deep into the ship's outer skin.

"It's time to abandon ship," Turok shouted as he jumped through another portal. Turok fell from the ship like a stone, and suddenly vanished into thin air. A second later, he landed in the dirt at the feet of his friends. At that same instant, the mine he'd planted on the mother craft exploded. *KA-BLAM!*

## Dedication

*For my friends Wally Green and Paul Kuhn of Gold Key Comics, the original keepers of the tales of Turok—m.t.*

# TUROK

## Way of the Warrior
### Adventure #1

Michael Teitelbaum

A GOLD KEY PAPERBACK
Golden Books Publishing Company, Inc.
New York

A Gold Key Paperback Original

Golden Books Publishing Company, Inc.
888 Seventh Avenue
New York, NY 10106

Copyright © 1998 by Golden Books Publishing Company, Inc.

Story by Fabian Nicieza and Michael Teitelbaum. Written by Michael Teitelbaum and Michael Morgan Pellowski. Additional concepts by David Dientsbier and Jeff Gomez.

Packaged for Gold Key Paperbacks by Town Brook Press.

ISBN: 0-307-16280-X

First Gold Key paperback printing November 1998

10  9  8  7  6  5  4  3  2  1

GOLD KEY® and design are trademarks of Golden Books Publishing Company, Inc.

Cover art by Art Staff Inc.: Ken Taylor
Flip animation by Charlie Botton

Printed in the U.S.A.

# Way of the Warrior

# Chapter 1

The vicious, reptile-like beast—known as a Fireborn—skittered across the cave floor. It sensed, rather than heard, the danger as an energy-charged Tek arrow whistled through the air. Despite its hulk, the Fireborn moved quickly. But it was too late. The arrow, a slender messenger of death, exploded upon impact as its tip punctured the scaly skull of the mutant dinosaur. A shower of warm, reptilian flesh splattered the cave walls. Steamy droplets of blood rained down upon Carl Fireseed, the man responsible for firing the Tek arrow.

The blood of the Fireborn was as hot as molten lava, as hot as the core of

Galyanna—an unearthly dimension, better known as The Lost Land, where Carl Fireseed now found himself doing battle. The Fireborn's blood would have roasted the tender flesh of any ordinary man, turning it the color of crisp bacon. The intense heat inside the cavern should have seared Fireseed's organs and charred his bones, but it did not.

Because Carl Fireseed was no ordinary man. He was a *Turok—Defender of Earth*. But right now he was about as far from his home planet of Earth as one could get.

*The Heart of Fire talisman has protected me once again*, Carl thought, as he fingered the sacred artifact and glanced at the burns on his flesh. *Without it, I would have instantly burned to death!*

Focusing once again on the beasts that surrounded him, Fireseed ignored the agony gnawing at his skin and sizzling in his guts. Instead he concentrated on fitting another energy-charged arrow to the string of his Tek bow. He whipped around just in time to target a Fireborn charging directly at him. He fired again. This time the chest of the charging Fireborn exploded. The mutilated creature fell to the dirt floor alongside the charred remains from others of his species.

Carl Fireseed stared at the smoldering

bodies. He thought of all the battles he had been in, all the creatures he had fought, since he took over the mantle of Turok from his brother. *During my time as Turok I have encountered all manner of despicable creatures in this interdimensional sewer called The Lost Land. But these Fireborn heavily outnumber me. They may be the deadliest foes I have yet encountered.*

Carl Fireseed laughed softly to himself, surprised at how calm and analytical his mind could be, even at a time like this. As a Turok he had learned to size up a situation before leaping into action. He watched now as a pack of Fireborn began to gather at the mouth of the cavern. Cut into the side of a volcano, the cavern served as a nursery. The incubator would soon be hatching young Dinosoids, deadly mutant dinosaurs.

Turok quickly surveyed his immediate surroundings. Within seconds he realized that his only escape path was blocked. The sight of Turok near their eggs was working the Fireborns into a savage frenzy. Smoke seeped from their sizzling pores and their whip-like tails lashed madly from side to side.

*No longer will they attack one by one,* Carl concluded.

He saw from the growing pack of Fireborns that the next charge against him would unleash a flood of flashing jaws and ripping claws.

*There will be no time to pick and choose individual targets. I need more firepower*, he decided quickly. Hurriedly he reached into the Light Burden, a fringed leather satchel that was slung over his shoulder. Sweat poured down his face as he concentrated intensely. Swiftly, he pulled an Autoshotgun out of the seemingly empty bag. The massive weapon could fire twelve continuous rounds of high-intensity bullets within seconds. He knew of few enemies who could withstand the assault from this weapon for more than a round or two.

Carl steadied himself as the first wave of Fireborns rushed toward him. A wall of teeth and claws closed in on the Protector of Earth. He leveled the Autoshotgun and squeezed the trigger. *BLAM! BLAM! KA-BLAM!* Dinosoid bodies shattered into fragments. *BLAM! KA-BLAM! BLAM!*

Roars of pain mixed with snarls of rage as reptile carcasses began to pile up before Turok. But this did not faze the bloodthirsty Fireborns. Their nursery had been invaded, and a million years of genetic instinct told them to destroy the intruder, whatever the cost. *KA-BLAM! BLAM! BLAM!* The Auto-shotgun continued to roar and take its deadly toll. But the Fireborns kept coming!

As Turok's eyes and hands trained on the savage adversaries before him, his thoughts turned to what had brought him into the burning bowels of The Lost Land. Why had he placed himself in such danger by tracking the Fireborns to their hidden lair? Why?

But he could no more escape the answer than he could escape the question: *I had to avenge the mass destruction by the Fireborn. I will never forget the sight of those innocent villagers, slaughtered for no apparent reason by a horde of Fireborn. My only hope for an answer was to invade this Fireborn nest.*

Carl laughed out loud as he thought of his father's wise words: *"Be careful what you hope for—it may come to pass."* I brought the Fireborn to me, all right, but there are far more of them than I ever imagined.

Turok continued to shoot until the cavern floor was piled high with dead and dying Fireborns. The walls and ceiling of the cave were soon plastered with thick, bubbling blood.

Turok fought harder than he ever had before. And with each new burst of energy the final words of a dying villager echoed through his mind: *Primagen has finally awakened!*

That terrifying thought consumed his mind while his highly-trained body continued to fight off the bestial onslaught. Carl Fireseed felt himself weakening. Darkness flickered at the edges of his consciousness. *I must stay conscious, must stay focused, or I have no chance at all.*

Turok began ticking off a mental checklist of facts to keep himself focused and awake. *Primagen. What do I know about Primagen?*

*I know that he is an incredibly powerful being from another universe. I know that because of some cosmic accident, he is responsible for the creation of The Lost Land. The aftermath of that accident threw together bits and pieces from random universes, which in turn formed The Lost Land.*

*I know that Primagen has been asleep, stuck in suspended animation, for centuries. I know that once conscious, he can use his telepathic powers to control the creatures of this place, forcing them to do his evil bidding. What else? What else? Oh yes! I know that his power is so great that he is capable of de-*

*stroying not only The Lost Land, but all universes that connect to it, including the one containing my precious Earth. His awakening spells doom for all living beings everywhere!*

With amazing control of both thoughts and body, Turok's brain continued to race while the Autoshotgun barked loudly and spewed round after round of death and destruction from its smoking barrel.

Turok's thoughts jumped to the Galyanna village that had been burned to cinders. Its occupants had been scattered, maimed, or brutally murdered by the Fireborn. *In all my time in Galyanna I have never heard of Fireborn traveling so far from their lair. Why have they senselessly raided the village?* he asked himself while effortlessly reloading the Autoshotgun.

The villager's final words again rang through his mind. *"Primagen has finally awakened!"*

*These creatures must have been ordered to the village through the telepathic power of Primagen. Ah, yes! And now I recall that the few surviving villagers referred to a mysterious, glowing pole that the Fireborn removed from the village. A totem, I believe they called it. But what does it have to do with Primagen?*

With the self-discipline of a true warrior, Carl instantly re-focused his attention on the terrifying danger before him. The largest and last of the Fireborns stomped toward him. The creature ignored the twisted and hideously contorted bodies of the other Dinosoids strewn in its path. It had but one thought in its thick, primitive skull: *Kill! Kill the intruder!* The monster hungered to sink its razor-sharp teeth into the soft flesh of the human.

"This is for the villagers who didn't survive your attack, Fireborn," Carl Fireseed stated solemnly. He raised the Autoshotgun to his shoulder. Slowly his finger curled around the trigger. He carefully aimed the sight of the weapon squarely over the heart of the mutant. His finger jerked backward. *BLAM! BLAM! BLAM!* Seemingly unending rounds of rapid-fire blasts tore into the Fireborn's body, hurling it up into the air while ripping it to bloody shreds.

At long last the battle was over. The danger had passed. There was nothing left to kill. Once again Carl Fireseed had survived despite the staggering odds against him. Or had he? He dropped to one knee and hastily examined his injuries. The Fireborn's lethal blood had burned deep into his upper torso.

Not even his protective Heart of Fire talisman had the power to keep him completely safe. Turok immediately realized the desperateness of his situation.

"I-I'm mortally wounded," he whispered without fear, remorse or regret. "I . . . I'm dying. . . ."

Slowly, Turok lifted a trembling hand to his forehead. He carefully flipped down the Folding Eye so that it was securely fastened over his right eye. The Folding Eye was a round eyepiece made of smooth black stone that allowed him to locate one of the many Fold Gate Openings, or pathways, to Earth. The portals were invisible to the naked eye. Never knowing when he might need an instant escape route to Earth, Turok kept the Folding Eye attached to the bandanna he wore wrapped around his head.

Gathering all of his remaining strength, Fireseed trembled as he lifted his arm. He peered through the circular eyepiece and spied one of the Fold Gate Openings near the rear of the Fireborns' cave. Clutching the Light Burden tightly, Carl Fireseed slowly rose up to his full height. His knees felt like they were going to buckle, but he refused to go down. Instead, as he had learned, he tapped inner reserves of strength and determination. Carl Fireseed steadied himself. He staggered toward the portal that would lead him to Earth . . . to Oklahoma . . . and to home. With a mighty leap he propelled himself through the portal doorway. His parting words to The Lost Land were slow and very direct.

"I must . . . get . . . to Joshua. He is our only hope now."

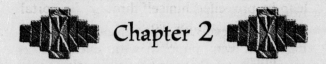

# Chapter 2

"Come on, Josh!" Coach Morgan shouted as Joshua Fireseed advanced slowly toward the plate with bat in hand. "Give that horsehide a ride. Send it! Show them where you live, kid!"

While a relief pitcher warmed up for the opposing team, Duke Morgan, the baseball coach of Central High School, stepped out of the third-base coaching box and walked toward the chain-link fence that enclosed Central High's home field.

Coach Morgan glanced up at the smattering of Central fans sitting in the bleachers. Among the supporters was

Barry Hackowitz. Barry was Joshua Fireseed's best friend. Josh and Barry were an odd pair of buddies, to say the least. Both were seventeen years old, but the similarities stopped there.

Josh Fireseed was tall, muscular, and athletic. He was popular with everyone at school, especially the young women. He was an average student, never seeing the need to tap the depths of his truly remarkable intelligence.

Barry Hackowitz, on the other hand, was openly brilliant and vocal. He was a skinny, intellectual type who wore big, thick glasses. Girls didn't pay much attention to Barry. In fact, they seldom even noticed the brainy president of the chess club. Nevertheless, the two mismatched opposites were inseparable pals. Maybe it was Barry's offbeat sense of humor, or maybe it was Josh's unswerving sense of loyalty, but Josh and Barry were best buds to the end.

"Smash one, Josh!" Barry yelled out to his pal, while pushing his drooping glasses along the bridge of his nose. "Plant it in the middle of the Oklahoma State campus. Right next to the girls' dorm!"

Coach Morgan didn't pay attention to Barry, or to any of the other cheering C.H.S.

fans in the stands. Right now all of Morgan's attention was focused on a middle-aged man sitting alone in the empty row of seats above the coaching box. Ken Matthews, the top scout for the Oklahoma State Comets, was wearing a yellow short-sleeved shirt and a gray Oklahoma State College baseball cap. On his lap was an open notebook. In his hand was a pen.

"I'm telling you, Ken, this Fireseed kid is a blue chipper," Duke Morgan called up to the scout. "He can do it all. He's a natural athlete. Last year he was All-Conference and All-Area at second base. This year I'm sure he'll be first team All-State. He has quick hands, great speed, and the power to send the ball into orbit. Just watch him at the plate."

Ken Matthews nodded as he scribbled some notes in his book. "He's a good-looking physical specimen for a seventeen-year-old," Ken agreed. "Do you think he can double as a second baseman and a shortstop in college? What Coach Atkins really needs is a hard-hitting infielder who can handle pressure."

"Josh is just what the doctor ordered," Duke Morgan professed. "He has a cannon for an arm. He could play shortstop. I honestly think there isn't a position on the field he can't play."

"And how is he under pressure?" Ken asked. "The game is on the line here. If he gets a hit you could qualify for the state playoffs."

"Fireseed is the very best I have," Duke Morgan answered without hesitation.

Ken Matthews nodded. He watched closely as Josh strolled up to the plate and prepared to hit with the bases loaded and two outs in the bottom of the fifth inning. Central High was down by one run. A lot was riding on the swing of the talented junior.

*Come on Josh, focus, focus,* Josh Fireseed told himself as he planted his right foot in the back of the batter's box. Then he cocked the bat over his right shoulder and set his sights on the burly relief pitcher brought in to face him. *I've creamed this guy the last two games I faced him. I don't know what is with me today. I just can't seem to catch up to his fastball.*

The opposing hurler stood at least six feet, four inches tall and weighed over two hundred pounds. His body had the dimensions of a human dinosaur. His thighs and biceps were huge. He returned Fireseed's icy stare.

There was no mystery about which pitch the reliever was going to throw. You didn't have to be Barry Hackowitz to figure out the plan. Everyone in the ballpark knew what was coming. It would be heat. The pitcher would try to smoke Fireseed with the fastball. The matchup was power against power.

"This should be very interesting," Duke Morgan said to Ken. Morgan took up his position as the third-base coach.

On the mound the opposing hurler began to work from a stretch. Fireseed tensed at the plate. The pitcher delivered a hard one, letter-high. Fireseed swung with all of his might.

"Strike one!" the umpire shouted as the horsehide thudded into the catcher's mitt.

"You're on it, Josh!" Duke yelled to his star player. "You're just a little late. Your swing needs to be quicker."

*What is wrong with me today?* Josh wondered again as he stepped out of the batter's box and wiped the sweat from his forehead. *It's like something is pulling at my brain, pulling my focus off the pitch. But what could be more important than being at-bat right now? Okay, stay calm, Josh, and focus. Focus!*

Joshua Fireseed collected himself and

rested his bat on his right shoulder. He looked down the third base line at his coach and nodded. Sweat poured from under his protective helmet as he got back into his batting stance.

The catcher flashed the pitcher a sign. The hurler smiled and went into his stretch. He delivered again. The pitch was another letter-high fastball that flamed its way from the mound to home plate. Joshua Fireseed swung. The bat tipped the ball, sending it back into the crowd of spectators.

"Foul ball!" the umpire cried. "No balls and two strikes is the count."

*I'm not gonna go down on strikes with the game on the line here, in front of the hometown fans and a college scout! Not me! Not the great Joshua Fireseed.* Josh stepped out of the batter's box again. For a moment he thought he heard a familiar voice calling his name. The voice seemed to echo inside his head, and for that one second there was no other sound, not the crowd, not the infield chatter of the opposing players. Nothing but the voice. And then it was gone. Josh glanced down at Coach Morgan, but the coach just flashed him a smile and a thumbs-up sign. *Man, this is weird. Come on, Josh, it's time to be Mr. Clutch!*

The ump crouched back down behind the

catcher. The pitcher was ready to deliver again.

Josh clenched his teeth and waited for what seemed like an eternity. He wanted an athletic scholarship to Oklahoma State so bad he could taste it. To gain the scout's respect all he had to do was smash the ball like he'd done so many times in the past.

*It's going to be the high fastball, Josh thought as he settled back into the batter's box. I know it's coming. All I have to do is whack it.*

The pitcher threw. Josh's bat swiftly whirled forward.

"Strike three!" yelled the umpire, as the pop of the ball hitting the catcher's mitt echoed around the field.

The catcher rolled the ball toward the mound and hustled off toward his own dugout. The pitcher smiled and strutted off the field.

Josh's jaw drooped toward his chest as he slammed his bat to the ground. He whirled around and stormed back to the bench. Kicking the chain-link fence behind the dugout, he disgustedly threw his batting helmet to the dirt.

"Of all days to lose my concentration!" he shouted at a curious

17

teammate. "And the crazy part is I can't even tell you what's distracting me!" The teammate looked at Josh strangely, then moved over to give him some space. It was obvious Josh wanted to stew in his own anger and disappointment.

"It doesn't look like the kid can handle big-time pressure, Duke," Ken Matthews said to the high school coach.

Coach Morgan sighed. "He just had a bad time at bat," he replied. "This Fireseed kid is something really special, believe me."

Duke Morgan walked up and joined Joshua at the bat rack near the fence. The young star stared at the tops of his shoes, his jaw clenched tightly. "I blew it, Coach," said Josh, still furious with himself. "I had a chance to really impress that scout and I blew it."

Coach Morgan put his hand on Josh's shoulder. "Don't sweat it. The game's not over. That's one good thing about baseball. The game has more than one inning. You usually get a chance to redeem yourself."

"Excuse me, Coach," someone yelled from behind the fence. "Should I give this to you?"

Both Coach Morgan and Josh looked around. Holding the foul ball Josh had tipped into the stands was Vivian

Jakashawah, Joshua's older, married sister. Josh and his fifteen-year-old sister, Alison, lived with Vivian, her husband Henry, and their two children, eight-year-old Clay and three-year-old Beth.

The Fireseeds and Jakashawahs lived on the Saquin reservation a few miles from Central High School. They were all members of the Saquin tribe.

Vivian flipped the baseball to Coach Morgan who caught it.

"It's nice to see you, Mrs. Jakashawah," the coach said. "I can't remember the last time I saw you at a game."

"You picked a great game to show up for, Viv," said Josh glumly. "Just in time to watch your baby brother screw up his entire future."

Vivian glanced at her brother. "As a matter of fact, it's your future that I've come to talk to you about."

"What do you mean?" asked Josh, feeling a little annoyed. "You came to watch me strike out in front of the Oklahoma State scout?"

"I'm not talking about your future as a baseball player, Josh," replied Viv quietly. "I'm talking about the family heritage. Your time has come."

"Now don't start with that stuff," snapped Josh. "I have to get out to my position."

Without warning, the voice inside Josh's head returned. And with it came the overwhelming knowledge that he had to go home with his sister. Despite all logic to the contrary, Joshua Fireseed felt compelled to leave the biggest game of his life for no apparent reason.

"What's the matter, Josh?" asked Coach Morgan. "You look pale. Are you all right?"

At that moment the umpire came over to the Central High dugout. "You're holding up the game, Coach," he said. "You've got to put a man out there to play second base."

Coach Morgan turned to Josh. "Can you stay in the game, son?" he asked.

Josh cupped his forehead in his hands. "I can't explain it, Coach," he muttered softly. "But I have to go. I don't understand it. I just have to leave." Then he turned and walked off the field.

"Yo! Josh! Where are you going?" Barry Hackowitz yelled from the bleachers. "It was only one at-bat. You'll cream him next time!"

Josh didn't answer his best friend. He just kept on walking.

"I thought I'd have to hit you over the head with a bat to get you to leave in the middle of a game," said Viv, as she walked alongside her brother.

"Don't rub it in," said Josh. The two got into Vivian's station wagon and sped off toward the Saquin reservation. "I can't believe I just did that, and I really don't know why I left, but I almost wasn't there today anyway. My concentration was way off. I stunk up the place. It's like something was grabbing at my brain. I-I, I don't know." Then turning to his sister he asked, "Why did you come for me, anyway?"

"I was wondering when you would get around to asking me that," Viv replied with a tiny smile. But almost instantly her tone changed. "It's Uncle Carl. He's come home." Her eyes met her brother's puzzled look. "He's not well. It's serious." She paused. "Do you understand? The mantle is about to be passed . . . to you!"

Josh stared silently at the dashboard.

Vivian shook her head. "We have to hurry," she said, keeping her expression perfectly blank.

After a few minutes Josh broke the uncomfortable silence. "Every time Uncle Carl comes around it makes me think of Pop."

Vivian sighed deeply at the mention of their father.

21

"I can't stop thinking about what a failure he was," continued Josh. "After today's performance I feel like I'm ready to follow in his footsteps. What's next for me—drinking, messing things up, and finally, the famous disappearing act without a trace?"

"What's next for you is waiting at home," replied Vivian. "You must speak with Uncle Carl while there is still time."

Josh slumped back into his seat and stared out the window. Silence once again filled the car.

Vivian wasted no time in getting Josh home. She knew that time was something Carl Fireseed was almost out of. As the car screeched to a stop outside the Jakashawahs' home, Henry and Clay were waiting in the open doorway.

"Hurry, Viv," Henry urged. "Carl is getting weaker with every passing minute. He needs to speak to Joshua before his time is up."

"What's going on?" Joshua demanded as his sister dragged him into the house.

Vivian ignored Josh's question and pulled Josh into the house. In the living room Cal Jakashawah, Henry's father, who was the mayor of the Saquin reservation, and Martin Sunhope, an elder historian of the Saquin tribe, greeted them.

"What is this, a tribal council meeting?" Josh asked flippantly.

"Well it sure isn't a surprise party for you, big brother," Alison Fireseed mocked. Josh turned to see his younger sister seated on a chair and holding three-year-old Beth on her lap.

Alison was decked out in her usual attire—ripped denim shorts and a black halter top—which revealed a striking red dragon tattoo that spread halfway across her shoulder and down her back. A single silver and turquoise earring dangled from her left ear. A nose ring sat in the middle of her right nostril. She stuck out her tongue at Josh as he passed by and he wondered for the hundredth time what had led her to get her tongue pierced. The silver stud that sat near the tip of her tongue reflected the light from a lamp in the corner of the room.

"This, Joshua Fireseed," began Martin Sunhope, "is an ancient Saquin ritual. It is a ritual that concerns your ultimate destiny."

Josh simply stared at the tribal elder. "Please spare me all the tribal mumbo jumbo," Josh answered. "Just tell me what this is all about."

"Your Uncle Carl will explain it to you," Martin said. He raised a time-ravaged, wrinkled hand and pointed to the half-open door that led to the spare room. "Go, Joshua Fireseed," Martin commanded. "Learn of your heritage. Accept your destiny. . . ."

Josh took a deep breath. He walked toward the door. All eyes were on him as he pushed the door open and peered inside. What he saw filled him with horror and revulsion.

Carl Fireseed was lying on a huge bear skin spread on the floor in the center of the room. His face, arms, and exposed body parts were covered with sores, oozing yellow pus, deep, discolored burns, and long, ugly lacerations. His torso was partially covered by a white sheet. The sheet was soaked through with blood. Near one side of Carl's head was a puddle, the contents of which Josh decided not to guess about.

Joshua cringed. The room smelled awful. The foul stench made his stomach twist into a knot. Josh didn't recognize the sickening scent. But Carl knew it was the aroma of death.

Josh turned. He wanted out of the room. "C-Close the door," Carl Fireseed said in a harsh, raspy voice. He rolled his head to look at his nephew. "My reign as Turok is nearing its end. Your time has come. I must pass the mantle to the firstborn Fireseed male."

"Huh?" Josh blurted out bluntly as he reluctantly eased the door shut. "Wha . . . ? What are you saying?"

"I-I'm saying the Turok legends of our tribe are true," Carl whispered. "For the last seventeen years I have been Turok, Protector of Earth."

Joshua folded his arms. "Right," he scoffed. "Of course you have, Uncle Carl. Tell me, did you capture the Loch Ness Monster or arm wrestle Bigfoot while you were busy being Turok?"

Carl Fireseed's eyes focused on the face of his nephew. His stare made Josh uneasy. "I-I'm sorry," Josh hurriedly apologized. "I didn't mean to mock you. You must be out of your head with pain. I'll get help." He turned to head for the door.

"No!" called Carl, shouting weakly. "Time is short. There are things I must tell you. They are things your father should have told you."

Joshua froze in his tracks. He spun on his heels. "My father? What does he have to do with this?"

"He . . . was . . . a . . . Turok," Carl said. He coughed, then his face contorted in pain. He spit up a big clot of blood. "Your father, John Fireseed, couldn't handle the pressure and demands of the task,"

25

Carl muttered. "Your father failed in his duty. That failure destroyed him as a Turok . . . and as a man. I was forced to step in and take his place."

Joshua inhaled deeply. *Was that why Pop drank? Why Mom left us? Could there be any truth in the wild ravings of a dying man? Was the Turok legend real and not just tribal myth?*

"Okay, so you're Turok," Josh said to his uncle. "I still don't see the connection here. What do you want with me? I have plans, big plans. I'm leaving the reservation. I'm going to win a baseball scholarship and go to Oklahoma State. Then I'm going to play in the big leagues."

Carl coughed and wheezed. His entire body trembled and his head shook uncontrollably. "Uncle Carl, I'd better get you a doctor," said Josh.

Weakly, Carl Fireseed raised his torso off of the floor. He propped himself up on one elbow. "Could a doctor mend the wounds inflicted by vile Fireborn Dinosoid blood?" he asked. He grabbed the edge of the sheet covering his torso. With a quick jerk he pulled the sheet away from his mutilated body.

Josh gasped. The flesh covering his uncle's torso had been almost completely torn away. Raw sinew and bare bone were visible.

Splintered ribs stuck out like slender bony fingers. Below the ribs, twisted coils of swollen intestines dangled out like yellow snakes yanked from a hiding place. Ruptured internal organs could be seen rotting inside the exposed abdomen and chest cavities.

Carl's body heaved with every feeble breath he inhaled. As his chest rose and fell, trying to suck air into his punctured lungs, fountains of blood gushed out of his body and onto the floor. Squirt by squirt, drop by drop, Carl Fireseed's heart was pumping itself dry of its life-sustaining fluid. Slowly, Carl covered his ghastly wounds with the sheet.

"For me the battle is over," Carl Fireseed said softly. "For you the war has just begun. You are the eldest male Fireseed of your generation. You are my successor."

Joshua began to shake his head slowly. "N-No," he mumbled. "No, I'm not. Even if the Saquin tales about the Turok legacy are true, I don't want any part of this. I have no training. I couldn't handle it. It destroyed my father! Look what it did to you." Josh shook his head rapidly. "Absolutely not! I-I'd just screw things up like my father did. I'm not the one you want. There's been a mistake! I can't be Turok," Josh insisted. "I am not Turok."

# Chapter 3

Once again Joshua Fireseed turned to leave the room. But with the determined strength of a dying man, Carl Fireseed reached over and grabbed one of his nephew's wrists. He held it in a vise-like grip, forcing Joshua to stop.

"Enough!" Carl shouted. He released Josh's arm and collapsed back onto the bear skin. He coughed up more blood. "Y-You cannot deny or refuse your birthright. The choice is not yours. This is not about you, me, or your father. It is about the protection and safeguarding of all of Earth."

The meaning of Carl's words slowly sunk into Joshua's brain. The least he could do

.

was listen. He knelt down beside his uncle. Carl shut his eyes momentarily, resting in the rootless place between life and death.

"I'm here, Uncle Carl," Joshua whispered. Gently he touched his uncle's shoulder. Slowly, Carl opened his eyes and began to speak.

"It is the destiny of the Fireseed lineage to protect Earth from attacks—attacks coming from a place called Galyanna, The Lost Land," Carl told Josh.

"Galyanna?" Josh repeated. "The Lost Land? Never heard of it."

"It is not in our universe," explained Carl. "Many of the creatures that live there are dinosaurs that have evolved into intelligent beings called Dinosoids. They are deadly enemies. A species of Dinosoid called Fireborns did this to me. But there are many kinds of Dinosoids as well as other beings in Galyanna. Most importantly they present a constant threat of discovering the openings that connect Earth to The Lost Land. That is why you must be Turok. You must continue to prevent this attack on Earth. Now the greatest threat Earth has ever faced has arisen. A creature who can destroy our entire universe has awakened in The Lost Land. You have to stop him."

"G-Galyanna? Dinosoids?" Joshua muttered in a puzzled tone. "I don't understand! I can't save the Earth. I can barely get a base hit."

"Here! Take this," Carl Fireseed ordered, ignoring Josh. He reached down under the sheet and removed a worn, fringed bag. "This leather satchel is known as the Light Burden," he stated. "It belongs to each Turok. Gaze into it deeply, Joshua Fireseed. Believe in yourself and it will assist you in your ensuing battles. It will also answer your questions." Carl paused. He was very weak. "Look into the Light Burden," he instructed, "and the legacy of Turok will be revealed to you."

Joshua took the satchel from his uncle's trembling hand. He held up the leather bag and examined it closely. It didn't seem very special. There was nothing extraordinary about it. It was just like many other Saquin heirlooms he'd seen passed down from generation to generation on the reservation. Josh opened the satchel and looked inside. *Give me a clue,* he silently begged the bag. But try as he might, all he found was an empty bag.

Josh scratched his head in puzzlement and shrugged his shoulders. "This empty old bag can't do anything for me, let alone Earth," he muttered. "Is it some kind of gimmick, like a magician's top hat?"

A look of anger flashed on Carl Fireseed's face. "The Light Burden has mystic powers that some consider magic, but it is no trick. Deepen your gaze into the bag, Joshua Fireseed, and concentrate hard. Now look!"

"Okay," Josh agreed. "Don't go ballistic. Stay calm. Your heart won't be able to handle it." Josh opened the satchel and peered inside. "I still don't see anything." He shook his head. "I'm telling you the truth, Uncle Carl. This bag is totally empty."

A faint smile appeared on Carl's cracked lips. "You are mistaken, nephew," he said. "The Light Burden is not empty. It is you who are empty."

"Look, I don't mean to be rude or anything, Uncle Carl," Josh muttered, "but I sure don't see what you're talking about." His mind wandered back to the game, and he wished he could leave the room right now and never look back.

"You must try to focus your thoughts and harness the power of your mind to achieve absolute concentration!" Carl demanded. He pointed a trembling finger at Josh's face. "Do it and do it now!"

The tone of his uncle's voice stunned

Josh. He nodded solemnly. He turned back to the satchel and began to focus his attention. His brow wrinkled as he steadied himself and concentrated. Joshua Fireseed couldn't believe his eyes. There was *something* in the bag. It was only a tiny glowing speck, but it seemed to be growing and swirling. It whirled faster and faster and faster! Suddenly, his eyelids felt heavy. He was drowsy. Josh felt a spinning sensation inside his head—as if his brain were caught in the vortex of a tornado. Everything started to go dim. He heard the voice that had called to him earlier. He recognized it now. It was the voice of his father. Then, instantly, an all-encompassing blackness swallowed him up.

Joshua Fireseed tumbled down, down, down through a funnel cloud, whirling through the space between our universe and all others. His weightless body sailed through one of the many portals that connected our universe to The Lost Land known as Galyanna.

*CRASH!* Joshua smashed into the top of a tall, leafy tree. Down he tumbled, branch after branch snapping under his weight. When he hit the ground he looked up and found himself staring into the small, beady eyes of a vicious Dinosoid. The hideous reptile hissed, and Josh sat frozen in terror and at the same time repulsed by the creature's foul breath.

The Dinosoid was no taller than Josh. Its skin was gray and cracked. Its head seemed too big for its body. It circled its prey, flashing two rows of razor-sharp teeth. The creature opened its huge jaws and lunged at Josh.

The young Turok rolled away from the Dinosoid's deadly jaws just as the spike-like teeth clamped shut on nothing but air. The frustrated creature circled Josh again, sizing him up and preparing for its next attack.

Josh looked around him and spotted a small branch from the tree he had crashed through. The branch was about the same size as a baseball bat. As the Dinosoid lunged again, Josh dove for the branch, grabbed it and rose to his feet, all in one smooth motion. He raised the branch over his right shoulder just as the furious creature attacked again. When the Dinosoid's head was just inches from Josh's face, the young, reluctant warrior swung the branch with all his might.

*CRACK!* The sound of the shattering Dinosoid's skull echoed through the trees. The creature collapsed in a heap at Josh's feet.

TUROK

"Now I get a hit," moaned Josh. "If only that guy's fastball was as big as this beast's head!"

"Dat wuz a nicesh job you did, kiddo," someone said to Josh. He looked up. The stranger's words were slurred and malformed, as if he'd been drinking. "We have t-thingsh to talk about, Josh."

Slowly the image of a man came into focus—a thin, raggedy scarecrow of a man. The haunting sight troubled Josh. Then he recognized the man standing before him. It was his father, John Fireseed, and he was holding the satchel Carl had given him.

"How do you like this place so far, kid?" John Fireseed asked, the slurring gone entirely from his voice. "This is Galyanna, or The Lost Land, if you prefer. Some people call it the interdimensional sewer of the universe. And I agree.

"Oh, you forgot this. Take it. It's yours now!" He threw the Light Burden at his son, hitting him in the face.

Josh grabbed the Light Burden and glared at his father. "What do you want?" he snarled. Questions of where he was or how his father had suddenly appeared were pushed to the back of his mind by his anger.

John Fireseed's voice became clearer and

34

stronger. "I know you hate me, son, for leaving you, your sisters, and your mother."

"I don't want your apologies," snapped Josh.

"I'm not here to apologize," replied John Fireseed. "I don't have the time to explain why I did what I did or where I've been. All I can say is that I can't change the past. All I can hope to do now is to assist in the future—your future." He pointed a bony finger at his son. "Maybe you can be the hero I couldn't be," he said. "Look into the bag again. Look, listen, and learn of the Turok legacy. Look, my son!"

Josh once again peered into the Light Burden. Strange images began to form in his mind's eye. The strange events that led to the formation of Galyanna, The Lost Land, began to unfold. He saw a huge spaceship, as big as a city, accidentally ripped from an alien universe into our universe. At the center of the enormous ship sat a being who seemed to be asleep. Josh then saw pieces of worlds ripped apart and drawn to this ship like lumps of clay thrown together to form a bizarre misshapen sculpture—Galyanna, The Lost Land. He saw the odd lifeforms that became part of Galyanna—hordes of dinosaurs, many of which had evolved into bizarre, intelligent life-forms, Dinosoids. These Dinosoids eventually thirsted for the conquest of Earth itself. He saw countless types of strange alien beings and monstrous mutations whose frightful appearance chilled him to the bone.

"It was one of our direct ancestors who, thousands of years ago, found a small glowing pocket of energy encased in amber. Without meaning to, he released the energy that opened the portals between Earth and Galyanna," John Fireseed explained to his son. "Because of this, it became an obligation of honor for the firstborn males of the Fireseed family to protect Earth from the deadly creatures of The Lost Land who might come through the portals. That original pocket of energy is now kept inside the Light Burden and is the source of its power.

"There have been many Turoks. I am the only one to fail in my duty. My brother Carl had to pick up the mantle so that Earth would not be destroyed." John Fireseed's voice became fainter. "I failed. You must not, my son." The last words he spoke were so soft Joshua barely heard them.

Josh looked up from the satchel. "Pop?" he called. John Fireseed was gone. Joshua was back in Vivian's house. He was kneeling beside his mortally-wounded uncle. The trance-like spell was broken. Joshua looked at Carl Fireseed. "Where is my father?" he demanded.

"H-He is dead," Carl mumbled. "But his spirit, like that of all Turoks, lives inside you."

Josh looked at the Light Burden with disdain. He tried to hand it back to Carl. "Take it," he said. "Give it to Vivian! Give it to Alison! Give it to Clay, for all I care! I don't want it."

Weakly, Carl shook his head. "It is for you, Joshua. It was always meant for you. Use it wisely," he instructed. "It will grant you access to an infinite number of weapons, magical objects, and powers." Carl wheezed. Blood started to stream out of his nostrils and ears. "Now . . . you . . . are . . . Turok . . . Protector of Earth!" Carl's eyes rolled back. His chest heaved violently one last time. His arms and legs quivered and then became forever still. Carl Fireseed's ordeal had finally come to a close. The mantle had been passed. For Joshua, the ordeal was just beginning.

Joshua Fireseed stood up. He stared at the Light Burden he was holding in his hands. "This can't be happening," he remarked in an astonished tone. "My uncle hands me an empty satchel and tells me to use it to protect the world? The way I see it, I've been left holding the bag!"

# Chapter 4

Martin Sunhope looked questioningly at Vivian Jakashawah. "Where is the new Turok?" Martin asked. "His training must begin immediately. Carl spoke of a new danger coming from Galyanna before he died. He didn't have the time to explain further. The new Turok must be prepared to face this ominous threat to Earth, whatever it is."

Vivian stepped in front of the stairs that led up to the second level of the Jakashawah home. She blocked Martin's path. "Joshua is in his room," she told the tribal elder. "But it's useless to try to talk to him. All he's done during the days since Carl's burial is sit on his bed and stare at the satchel. It's like he's in a trance. He won't go out. He won't pick up a baseball. He won't even speak to the girls who call him on the phone." Vivian shook her head. "I'm really worried about him," she confessed. "His behavior is starting to remind me more and more of the way Dad acted before he left the reservation."

"Do not worry," Martin consoled Vivian. "Joshua has not yet fully accepted his burden. In a day or two he will embrace his fate and shoulder his responsibility." The old Saquin historian nodded solemnly. "Joshua Fireseed has the blood of many courageous ancestors flowing through his veins. He will not turn his back on his ultimate destiny."

Vivian sighed. She wanted to believe in what Martin said. "I hope you're right, Martin," she replied. "Even Alison is worried about him. Of course she won't admit it, but she is! She keeps trying to think of a way to get him to snap out of his solitary confinement." Viv glanced up at the closed door at the top of the stairs that was the entrance to Josh's room. She turned and looked Martin right in the eyes. "What will we do if Josh refuses to accept his responsibilities?" She glanced behind her. Her eight-year-old son, Clay, was seated on the living room floor, watching television. "Clay is next in line," she said. "He's too young for the job. Who will become Turok?"

Martin put a hand on Vivian's shoulder. "Do not fret," he said softly. "I have faith in your brother. Now let's have some coffee," he suggested. Vivian nodded. Together they walked off toward the kitchen.

Upstairs in his room, Josh sat cross-legged on his bed. His elbows were propped up on his knees. His chin was in his palms. The fringed satchel was lying on the bed beside him. Josh was staring at the mystical pouch.

"This has all got to be a bad joke," he mumbled. "It's a hoax or something. It can't be real." He shook his head. "My Uncle Carl tells me my father was a Turok and messed up on the job. Then he tells me that *he* took over as Turok and was killed in the line of duty battling some kind of bizarre creatures called Fireborn Dinosoids."

Josh jumped off his bed. He began to pace the floor as he absentmindedly continued to talk to himself. "Sure! What Saquin kid hasn't heard about the great and mighty Turok, the legendary hero? I know the stories and myths as well as anyone." He continued to pace. "But Turok is only a legend like Hercules or Ulysses. There is no real Turok! There can't be!" He shook his head. "I must be going crazy. That is the only explanation. And everyone around here—Martin, Viv, and Henry—they're all crazy too. They keep talking about training me as if the Saquin reservation is some sort of Turok boot camp." He whipped a hand to his forehead in a mock salute. "Private Joshua Fireseed, a.k.a. Turok, Protector of Earth, reporting for duty, sir!"

Josh gritted his teeth. He glared at the Light Burden lying on his bed. "Ha!" he cried in exasperation. "How can I protect the world with an old leather sack that makes me hallucinate?"

Josh looked away from the satchel. "They had to be hallucinations," he muttered. "I couldn't have really seen or done any of those things. How could it be possible for me to travel to another universe, smack a Dinosoid's skull as if it were a homer, and then have a conversation with my dead father? Seeing Uncle Carl's horrible wounds must have affected my mind and caused me to space out." He nodded. "I freaked. That's all this is—an episode—a dream."

Josh sat down on his bed beside the Light Burden. He picked it up in one hand. Just touching it gave him a funny sensation.

There was something odd about the ancient pouch that he couldn't deny or resist. Now every time he held it, Josh felt a faint surge of power pulsating through his body. It was as if the Light Burden were calling out to him. There was no sensible or logical way to explain how he felt. It was as if he knew the satchel belonged to him. He was growing more and more connected to it.

Suddenly, there was a loud knock at the bedroom door. Josh ignored it at first. But the knocking persisted. Josh looked up. "Who is it?" he grumbled angrily.

"It's that publisher's sweepstakes thing with a ten-million-dollar check for Joshua Fireseed," his sister Alison responded mockingly. "Is Joshua Fireseed home?"

Joshua scowled. "I don't have time for you or your jerky jokes. Find a space on one of your ears that hasn't been pierced yet and go puncture it. I'm sure one of your tragically hip friends will be glad to do the job for free. So beat it! I'm busy."

"Chill out, big bro," Alison called back. "I'm not here to bug you. I know you've got a lot on your mind since Uncle Carl died." She paused to knock on the door again. "Open up. I've brought the prisoner a visitor from the outside world. He needs to speak to his long-lost blood-brother. This visitor won't take no for an answer."

"Yo! Open up, dude!" another voice called. Joshua recognized the voice. It was Barry Hackowitz.

"What are you doing here, guy?" Josh asked. Hearing Barry's voice cheered him up. Josh slid off the bed. He walked over, unlocked his door, and yanked it open. Standing before him in the hall was a smiling Barry and a sneering Alison.

"I bring you a pardon signed by the governor, bud," Barry said as he walked in. "The truth is," he continued, "Coach Morgan sent me over to check up on you. Your sister Viv called him and told him you weren't feeling well. I've been worried about you, too."

"I'm feeling fine," Josh countered. "I'm just a bit confused about things." Barry sat down on Josh's bed and eyed the Light Burden. Alison scooted into her brother's room before he could close the door and shut her out. Once again she stuck out her pierced tongue as she slipped past.

"That's it!" Alison said to Barry, pointing at the satchel on the mattress. "That's the family heirloom I told you about."

Barry picked up the Light Burden and examined it.

"Hey!" shouted Josh as he rushed toward the bed. "Don't fool with that!"

"See," Alison called. "I told you. He's obsessed with that old bag. He thinks it has magical powers or something. I heard him call it a mystical link between parallel dimensions. Josh is losing his grip, Barry."

Josh snatched the satchel out of Barry's hands. Barry nervously fidgeted with his glasses. Then he combed his hand through his short, unruly blond hair. "Hmmm. I suppose it is remotely possible for a link between simultaneous dimensions to exist in the form of a physical object like the bag, but that prospect is highly unlikely," he remarked.

Josh ignored his brainy friend's outburst. "Yeah, sure," muttered Josh. "But I can't get the darned thing to work again. I have to prove to myself that I didn't imagine all those things I saw and did." Josh reached his hand into the bag, fished around inside, then pulled out an empty hand. "See!" he announced. "No prize."

"Doesn't that thing come with any documentation?" kidded Barry. "No instruction manual or website address to check out?"

"Cute," replied Josh, suppressing

back a small smile. Barry could almost always get a chuckle out of his best buddy.

"Seriously, didn't your uncle give you instructions on how to operate this so-called interdimensional link?" Barry inquired.

"I think my uncle was a bit delusional at the end," Josh said. "I kept hearing voices and seeing things, but now I think it was all a demented form of hysteria induced by him."

"Talk about delusional," Alison remarked as she plopped down on Josh's bed. She casually glanced at her fingernails, which were painted black. She pointed an accusing finger at her brother. "Ask Josh who Turok is."

"Turok?" repeated Barry.

"Yeah, Turok—the Protector of Earth according to Saquin legend," Alison explained.

"Oh, *that* Turok," Barry said as if he understood, which he didn't. "I thought you meant *Buck Turok,* that guy who used to play third base for the Mets." He looked at Josh. "So, big fella, who is Turok?"

Josh pointed a finger at the middle of his chest. "I am," he announced. "At least that's what a lot of people around here keep telling me." He sighed. "And as Turok I'm supposed to do astounding things with this bag." He held up the Light Burden.

Alison glanced at Barry and made a gesture that indicated she thought her brother had gone nuts. Barry looked away and focused his attention on his best friend. "Didn't your uncle give you a clue about how to use the bag?" he asked.

Josh thought for a second. "He told me to concentrate hard and to believe in myself," he answered, as he opened the Light Burden. He held the satchel up with one hand and shut his eyes tightly.

"Hey, guys," Alison called out. "Maybe we should click our heels together three times and say 'There's no place like Galyanna. There's no place like Galyanna.' Or maybe we should hold a séance. Maybe we all have to hold hands to make it work," she joked. Alison reached out to grab Josh's and Barry's hands. Josh held one edge of the Light Burden. Barry touched the other edge of the open bag. As soon as his fingertips touched the edge of the leather satchel, the three kids formed a mystical connection.

Josh opened his eyes and peered into the satchel. Something seemed to be swirling inside. The sight mesmerized him. His concentration intensified. Without warning, Josh, Barry, and Alison were violently pulled into the Light Burden, sucked into a whirling vortex that whisked them into the open portal between two dimensions, two worlds.

*WHOOSH!* Their unexpected exit from Earth was instantaneous and terrifying.

"Nooo!" shrieked Alison as they plummeted through the dimensional opening.

Downstairs, Clay had just switched off the TV. He heard Alison's scream and dashed up to Josh's room to see what was going on. He halted at the unlocked door and slowly pushed it open. Then he rubbed his eyes in disbelief. The room was empty. The windows were all closed. There was no other way to leave the house except through the living room door. But the trio, and the ancient fringed satchel known as the Light Burden, had definitely vanished!

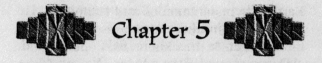

# Chapter 5

*S*PLASH! SPLISH! SPLOSH! One by one, the three terrified travelers had been ripped suddenly from one dimension and plunged into the murky water of a putrid primordial pool of another. As their heads bobbed to the surface of the muck and they gasped for breath, alarming questions seeped into their brains.

"What happened? How did we get here?" Alison sputtered.

"Where are we?" Barry demanded. "I hope we purchased round-trip tickets!"

"Why?" Josh called out in an ago-nized voice. "Why is this happening again?"

Alison groaned as she began to tread water. "Ick! This place smells like a sewer."

"I-If we're where I think we are, it's the sewer of the universe," Josh answered.

"W-Where is that?" Barry mumbled. He spit out a mouthful of scum-covered water.

"Let's get to the shore first," Josh said, glancing around. "It's not far. We can try to make sense of this once we're on dry land." Josh slipped the strap of the Light Burden over his shoulder. Once it was in place he began to swim toward shore. Alison followed, with Barry behind her.

"You call this dry land?" Alison complained as she pulled herself through ankle-deep slop. Josh yanked his sister and friend further away from the water's edge. They plopped down to rest on a thick cushion of moss hidden beneath a tall curtain of giant ferns.

"This flora is totally weird," Barry said while regaining his breath. "There are palms and giant ferns mixed with mutated conifers and twisted hardwoods." He glanced around. "This place looks like the creation of some insane alien horticulturist."

Alison wiped pond scum off her legs. "Someone around here is insane," she agreed. "I just hope it's not me." She eyed her brother, who was sprawled on the ground. He sat up and returned her accusing stare.

"Don't look at me!" he snapped. "I warned you two not to fool with the satchel." He patted the Light Burden hanging at his side. "I told you this thing was no toy."

Barry turned serious. "So the bag really is a link to another dimension," he announced in astonishment. "We've been teleported to another world."

"A Lost Land," Josh added. "*The* Lost Land of Galyanna."

"Well, pardon me for not applauding," said Alison. "Galyanna, huh? Humph! I didn't enjoy the trip very much and the landing was a total bummer." She pointed at the satchel. "You didn't happen to pack any of those towelette things in there, did you? I'd kinda like to tidy up before we're served our in-flight meal."

"Harr! Harr!" mocked Josh. "Very funny."

Barry tapped Josh on the shoulder. "Now, you know that I'm usually Mr. Big Yuks," began Barry. "Good old 'Laugh-A-Minute' Hackowitz, that's me. But I don't think there's anything funny about that!"
Barry pointed at the lake they'd just climbed out of. Water near the surface

51

was bubbling, foaming, and churning as if something deep in its depths were rising.

As the three reluctant visitors watched in awe, a huge reptilian head emerged from the greenish foam. First came the bony crown of the beast's head, followed by two glowing, red eyes, two huge nostrils spewing sprays of water, and then a set of horrible gaping jaws. The behemoth bellowed, revealing two rows of long, sharp teeth.

"I'm dreaming," Alison said. "Please, tell me I'm dreaming. That can't be a dinosaur."

The gigantic head rose higher and higher at the end of a long, serpentine neck.

"A-Actually," corrected Barry, "it doesn't look like any kind of dinosaur species I'm familiar with. It's some kind of strange reptilian mutant."

"Will you two please shut up," whispered Josh. "It's called a Dinosoid, okay? And it's got big teeth! Fortunately, it hasn't seen us yet."

Frozen by fear, the three accidental tourists became silent. They watched in tense terror as more of the beast's scaly gray-green body rose to the surface.

"Let's try to sneak away," Josh whispered very softly, his voice shaking. He watched as the creature in the lake slogged toward the shore.

"It's coming!" squealed Barry in a choked whisper.

"Some Turok you are," Alison said quietly as she crept on her hands and knees next to her brother. "We're squirming away in muck like cowardly worms."

"Just be quiet and keep squirming," Josh ordered. Alison wiggled through the ferns and reeds, moving deeper and deeper into the lush undergrowth.

"Josh is right," Barry acknowledged as he scooted past his friend. "A wise warrior knows when to run and when to fight."

Josh stayed behind, keeping his eyes on the monster. "Uhh . . . this might be a good time to start running!" he shouted suddenly. "That thing just spotted us!"

The towering Dinosoid turned its long neck in the direction of Joshua, Barry, and Alison. Its mouth opened and a blood-chilling growl erupted from its throat. Instantly, Barry and Alison jumped to their feet.

"Come on, Josh! Make a run for it!" Barry urged. He and Alison began to thrash frantically through the foliage.

"We'll never make it," Josh shouted. "Keep going. I'll try to distract it." He gulped. "Even though I'm not sure how," he muttered as the lumbering beast splashed toward him.

"No! Josh! Don't!" Alison screamed as Barry pulled her away.

"Uncle Carl told me this satchel is a mystical doorway to an arsenal of weapons," Josh muttered again. He swallowed hard and thrust his hand deep into the Light Burden hanging at his side. He concentrated with all of his might. "I could sure use some type of cosmic ray gun or phaser blaster," he shouted as the monster thundered closer.

Sweat poured down his face. He stood steadfast against the mad charge of the prehistoric mutant. Josh tried his best to believe in himself and the mystic power of the Turok lineage. "That baseball scout should see me now," Josh muttered. "Talk about 'Big Game Situations.'" He smiled and yanked a Tek bow along with a handful of Tek arrows out of the satchel. His grin quickly faded.

"Huh?" Josh sputtered as he eyed the weapons. He gulped. "It's no ray gun, but I guess it will have to do!" Josh looked closely. "There is something different about this bow and these arrows," he said as he fitted an arrow to the string of the bow. "They look more high-tech than the bows and arrows I've fired before, but at least it's a weapon I know how to use."

The brave Saquin youth stretched the string to his ear, aimed, and fired the arrow. "Who says Joshua Fireseed can't handle pressure!" Josh grunted as the slender shaft whizzed toward its tiny target: the right eye of the great beast.

*SPLURT!* The energy-charged arrow hit its mark, passing through the creature's milky white eyeball, then detonating. The monster bellowed in pain as its tiny brain exploded inside its skull, killing it instantly. Then the hulking, gray-green reptile toppled like a felled tree and landed with a great splash. Its scaly skin disappeared beneath the water's surface as it slowly sank to the bottom of the lake.

Josh slipped the Tek bow and arrows back into the Light Burden, where they disappeared into the bottomless sack.

"Did you see that?" Barry gasped as he pointed toward the scene of the fallen Dinosoid. "D-Did you see what Josh just did? What did you call him back in his room—Turok, Protector of Earth? Well, he just did a bang-up job of protecting our butts from certain death."

"I did it," Josh whispered softly to

himself. Then in a louder voice he repeated, "I did it!" He turned and rushed off toward Barry and Alison. "Did you see that?" he called out as he approached. "I don't know exactly how I did that, but I did it."

Joyfully, Barry clasped his arms around Josh's shoulders. Together they bounced up and down, gleefully patting each other on the back as they had done so many times before when Josh had smacked a game-winning homer.

"Enough with the male bonding already," Alison said, as she stood there with her arms folded. "Problem One solved by Turok, our hero," she admitted. "By the way, nice job, Josh. But what about Problem Two? How do we get out of this miserable place? I, for one, have tickets for the Marilyn Manson concert tomorrow night, and I really don't want to miss it!"

Josh turned to Alison. "I'm not really sure how to get us home," he admitted. "But I'm open to suggestions."

Alison pointed at the satchel. "Maybe there's a return ticket home in the bag," she said. "You found the bow and arrows in there when you needed them." Alison looked around and shivered. "We need to get out of here. See if the bag will teleport us home," she suggested. "This place really gives me the creeps." Alison glanced at the thick, steamy jungle at the edge of the marsh. It was filled with eerie noises, strange plants, and terrible smells.

"I'll try," Josh promised. Then he opened the Light Burden and looked inside. He concentrated so hard that beads of perspiration popped out on his brow. But try as he might, nothing happened.

"Sorry, Sis," Josh said sincerely. "It's not working." Alison exhaled loudly.

"Why don't we try another séance?" asked Barry. "It worked to get us here."

Josh shrugged. "Why not?" he replied.

The three friends held hands and touched the edges of the Light Burden as they had in Josh's room. Nothing happened this time.

"It's not working," sighed Josh. "It's just not the same. Maybe I'm really supposed to be here in Galyanna, and not on Earth and that's why it's not sending us home. Maybe there's more to this destiny stuff than I originally thought. I don't know."

A look of dismay appeared on her face. Josh went up to his sister and put an arm around her. "Don't worry," he consoled. "We'll find our way home. Until then, I won't let anything happen to you or Barry."

Alison nodded and flashed Josh a weak smile. She gave her brother a quick peck on the cheek. "Thank you, Mighty Hero," she said softly.

"Um," began Barry, "I hate to bust up this tender family moment, but I actually have tickets to the Marilyn Manson concert too, and I—"

Barry stopped mid-sentence as his astonished friends looked on.

"All right, so they're really tickets to the Computer Expo," admitted Barry, beginning to laugh. Alison and Josh joined in and the three laughed so hard they had to wipe tears from their eyes. After a few minutes Barry regained his composure and added, "But I want to get home just as badly as Ali does."

"Then let's find a way out of Galyanna," announced Josh, finally shaking off his laughter.

"Lead on, mighty Dinosoid slayer," Alison urged, as the last of her giggles died down. Josh slung the Light Burden over his shoulder and began to tramp through the underbrush. His friend and sister followed his lead.

The trio wandered around aimlessly for hours. For all they knew, they could have been going in circles. They had no way of knowing which direction was right and which direction was wrong. They didn't even know if there were right or wrong directions in this bizarre place.

"It's hopeless," Alison finally admitted. She sat down on a rotting tree stump in a tiny clearing. "We're lost and starving." She looked at the Light Burden slung over her brother's arm. "I'd swap that mystical satchel for a picnic basket in a heartbeat," she admitted.

"Me too," said Josh. He glanced over at Barry who was seated on a fallen log and staring straight up at the sky through a break in the treetops.

"What do you see?" Josh asked.

"Is it food?" Alison asked gingerly. "Fruit or nuts?"

"It's a bird," Barry answered. "I see a big bird. It's circling right over us."

Josh put a hand over his eyes to shield them for a better look. "That is one huge bird," he said, "and it's way up there." Josh got to his feet. "Let's keep going," he said. "Sitting here just isn't going to get us anywhere." Alison and Barry stood up. Wearily they followed Josh into the woods. A short time later they entered a large open meadow.

"At least we're out of the woods, literally," Alison said.

Barry gazed skyward. "Look!" he said as he pointed upward. "That bird is still with us."

Just then the huge bird broke through the clouds and began to dive toward them. Gradually Barry saw it more clearly.

"That's not a bird," yelled Barry in alarm. "It's a giant flying reptile—a Pteranodon—or whatever Dinosoid creature the Pteranodon has mutated into, in this crazy place!"

The winged Dinosoid streaked out of the heavens and dove toward the defenseless trio standing in the center of the clearing. The mutated Pteranodon screeched ferociously as it bulleted its prey.

"Quick! Hit the dirt!" Josh shouted. He shoved Alison to her knees and dropped to the turf himself. Alison tumbled into the tall grass as Barry dove headfirst onto the ground.

The Pteranodon swooped low. Its sharp talons caught the edge of Barry's shirt and tore the right sleeve off. "Ahh!" screamed Barry as the monster climbed and prepared to dive again.

"We're dead ducks caught out in the open like this," Barry said, looking at his shredded shirt. "And I was going to wear this shirt to the Computer Expo, too. Good thing

I won't be home in time!" He shuddered, then crawled through the tall grass toward Alison.

"We're not dead ducks and we're not sitting ducks—either," Josh answered boldly. He rolled on his back and grabbed for the Light Burden. His sister and friend cowered behind him as he reached into the satchel. "I promised I wouldn't let anything happen to you, Sis," Josh swore, "and I meant it." He yanked a huge rifle out of the satchel. It was a tranquilizer gun.

"What is that?" Barry asked.

"I'm not sure," Josh answered, peering into the barrel of the rifle. "But it looks like it fires some type of darts." Josh raised the rifle to his shoulder. The Pteranodon was just beginning its second dive. Josh got to a kneeling position to fire. He squeezed the trigger.

*BLAM! WHOOSH!* A tranquilizer dart zoomed through the air heading for the flying Dinosoid. But the creature moved quickly, shifting its flight path. The dart zipped past it and its dive continued.

This time Josh was the target. Razor-sharp talons flashed inches from his face. The young Turok twisted out of the way, but the talon scraped Josh's shoulder and caught hold of the Light Burden! The

61

beast soared skyward with the satchel firmly in its grip.

"Are you all right!" shouted Alison, as she jumped to her brother's side.

"It's just a scratch," said Josh, looking at the small trickle of blood on his shoulder. "But that thing has the Light Burden. I can't believe it! I've been a Turok for all of a week, and already I've lost the one thing that has been passed down from Turok to Turok for thousands years!"

"You've still got the gun," Barry reminded his friend.

"That's right," said Josh firmly. He raised the weapon and sighted his target. "This time I need to anticipate his flight. Lead the shot a bit." Then he gently squeezed the trigger.

The second tranquilizer dart streaked into the sky and this time it struck the Pteranodon in its long, slender neck. The winged reptile screeched and somersaulted tail over beak. Its massive, leathery wings began to flap as the effect of the tranquilizer took a stranglehold on its muscles. The monster's limbs jerked spasmodically and then froze. The beast plummeted out of the sky like a stone and crashed loudly into a grove of trees at the opposite side of the meadow with the Light Burden still in its grasp.

"Good shot," complimented Barry. "You *bagged* the Pteranodon, so to speak."

Alison got up. She joined Barry and Josh as they moved toward the motionless monster. The great winged reptile remained frozen as they cautiously crept closer to it.

"I-Is it dead?" Alison asked.

Josh shook his head. "I don't know," he answered. The creature's chest heaved up and down with a weak breath. "It's just knocked out," Josh said as he carefully unhooked the Light Burden's shoulder strap from the beast's talon. He patted the bag that once again hung by his side. Then he slipped the tranquilizer gun into the satchel. The weapon returned to its place in the mystic, unseen Turok arsenal. "I think we'd better be moving on before our stunned friend wakes up."

"Which way?" Alison asked in a puzzled tone.

"This way," called Barry. He waved his friends over. "There's a narrow path here. It leads into the forest."

"Do you think it leads to a way out of The Lost Land?" Alison asked.

"The only way to find that out is to follow it," said Josh. "Let's go."

"Why not?" Alison agreed. "What do we have to lose . . . besides our lives, the Light Burden, and a little blood?"

Josh shot her a glance as he wiped the small trickle of blood off his shoulder.

"All right! All right! Just joking!" Alison shot back.

The narrow trail twisted through a thick, eerie forest. The trio of travelers passed dense vegetation that seemed totally alien to them. Most of the plants were unrecognizable even to Barry's trained scientific eye.

"Remind me never to recommend this place as a tourist resort," said Alison as they stumbled along. She pushed a dangling vine out of her path.

Strangely, the vegetation they passed started to thin. It was as if someone or something had trimmed it back to a comfortable level. As they proceeded along the trail, the foliage continued to dwindle. They could now see the tops of distant cliffs.

The trio halted at the last sparse remnants of woodland and peered out over a barren stretch of landscape. Before them stood a bleak desert plain. The path led through the desert and ended by circling around a huge, strange-looking mound.

"Whoever cut this trail used some type of powerful defoliant to kill all the surrounding plants," Barry explained. He glanced out at the towering mound of dirt in the distance. "And it's not a natural formation," he said. "It was done on purpose."

"It reminds me of a gigantic anthill," Josh remarked.

"It looks more like a big beehive," Alison said, pointing to the mysterious mound. "There's something moving around inside there," She strained her eyes to get a better look. "It looks like some type of little insects, like aphids or ants."

"I think they just look small from here," Barry explained. "Up close they're probably as big as men."

Josh nodded. "Great, first Dinosoids and now man-sized alien aphid-ants. I think we should call them 'Mantids,'" he added. "Just so we know what we are talking about when we laugh about all this later over a pizza or two back in Oklahoma."

"Make mine mushroom," said Barry. "I'm starving."

As they continued to watch, the worker Mantids busied themselves around the hive. They were very industrious and seemed peaceful enough.

"I'm going to risk approaching the

65

hive," Josh said finally. "Maybe I can communicate with those Mantids."

"What about us?" Alison inquired.

"You two wait here just in case there's trouble," Josh ordered.

"That suits me," Barry acknowledged honestly. Alison glared at him. Barry fiddled with his glasses. "Well, it does," he said.

"Now stay put," Josh commanded. He started out from behind their sparse cover. "Keep low and out of sight. Whatever happens don't come after me."

"Playing the hero again, Turok?" Alison asked.

He stared at his little sister. "No," he responded. "I'm just doing what has to be done."

Alison then reached out and touched her brother's arm. "Be careful, Josh," she told him.

"Take care of yourself, Bud," Barry instructed. "Without you, we're dead meat."

"I'll be back," Josh promised. "And in one piece." He tugged on the Light Burden slung over his shoulder. "If I get into trouble, I'll use this."

Boldly, Josh started out toward the Mantids' hive. He walked slowly and didn't make any threatening gestures. He kept his arms and hands in plain sight. Step by step he inched closer and closer to the hive. "I just hope they don't think I'm some kind of door-to-door exterminator," he whispered jokingly to himself.

Josh was just about halfway to the alien structure when the worker Mantids became agitated. They scurried about in a frenzy and began to emit a piercing whine that caused Josh's ears to buzz. Sensing a greater danger, he halted.

Seconds later, some new, larger Mantids appeared in the sky above the hive. The larger Mantids had jet packs strapped to their backs which they skillfully used to propel themselves through the air. The new Mantids were deadly and dangerous four-armed drones.

The drones began to whirl above the hive in an angry swarm. Josh watched in awe as the flying Mantids gradually formed ranks in the sky. They were preparing to attack. Josh studied the four-armed insects carefully. His eyes widened in shock and alarm. Clasped in their insect extremities were some type of guns.

"I'm trapped out here in the open without any cover," Josh muttered to himself. "If they open fire on me with their guns I won't stand a chance of surviving. I need protection."

Joshua turned to the Light Burden. Frantically he reached inside the satchel searching for something that would shield his body from the force of the Mantids' weapons. From deep in the bag Turok pulled out two mysterious pieces of apparel.

One was a magical, protective chest plate. Josh slipped the breastplate over his head and hung it around his neck. It dangled down in front of his torso and covered his tattered T-shirt. Instantly, instinctively, Josh knew that the wood-and-rawhide-laced breastplate carried the imbued essence of the Saquin *Bear Spirit* and would make its wearer impervious to physical harm. Whether the spirit of his ancestors—the Turoks that came before him—were communicating with him on some unconscious level or the knowledge of the power of the breastplate was in the shield itself, Josh was not sure. But he knew it would keep him from harm.

The other article of clothing he removed from the satchel was a fringed pair of leather chaps. He quickly strapped the chaps to his jeans. Once again the knowledge came to him that the chaps would improve his natural reflexes and vastly increase his foot speed. Josh knew that at last he was wearing the attire of a Turok, Protector of Earth.

Strangely satisfied, he turned his attention back toward the sky. Three scout Mantid drones were jetting away from the hive and streaking toward him. He sensed danger yet he didn't want to appear hostile. He refrained from drawing a weapon of any kind from the Light Burden.

"I come in peace!" Josh shouted as he raised his empty palms to the sky. "I carry no weapons." The drones headed right for him and leveled their guns. "I don't want trouble!" Josh hollered.

The drones ignored his overtures of peace and aimed their weapons at the young Turok. The first drone fired.

*ZAP!* An energy blast hit Josh squarely in the chest and was deflected off of his breastplate. The shot left him physically unharmed, but it hurled him backward. He ended up sprawled in the dust. A moment passed before the dazed hero could stagger to his feet.

*ZAP! ZAP!* The other drones opened fire without warning. Josh quickly regained his balance. He tumbled forward and then rolled from side to side to avoid the gauntlet of deadly blaster fire.

Young Turok faced his attackers. Enraged, he waved a clenched fist at his airborne adversaries. "I came in peace, but if it's a fight you want, so be it!" he declared.

The flying alien insect scouts prepared to attack again. The rest of their fellow warriors remained in a protective defensive formation above the hive. The scouts didn't seem to need any help.

*ZAP! ZAP! ZAP!* The drones rained lethal fire down on Joshua Fireseed. As he raced around dodging the deadly blasts, he reached into the Light Burden and yanked out a long silver tube with a large opening on one end. Unbeknownst to Josh it was one of the Turok's most devastating weapons—the Cerebral Bore!

Josh dropped to one knee to inspect the weapon in his hand. *What is this?* He stared into the open end of the tube, spying a silver projectile. *But where's the trigger?* Josh ran his hand along the length of the weapon. Its surface was smooth. *Maybe there's something else I can use in here.* Josh plunged his hand back into the Light Burden.

Josh felt his mind focus. All noise and unnecessary thought were blocked out and the answer became clear. Instead of pulling out another weapon, he aimed the silver tube

70

at the swarm of Mantid drones and united all his thoughts into one single theme: ATTACK!

Instantly, three silver metallic projectiles shot skyward. The projectiles homed in on the brainwaves of the three drones. No matter how fast they flew or what evasive courses they chose, the targets could not evade the projectiles or alter their ultimate fate.

One by one the projectiles found their marks and locked a set of hooked prongs onto the head of each Mantid drone. The prongs thrust deep into the insects' skulls upon impact.

Instantly, a fountain of blood and brain fluid gushed out of the bore holes as the victims' life fluids were jettisoned from their wounds.

The first drone flew out of control and smashed to the ground. Right before he plummeted to the dust, the bore projectile fell out, dropped to the ground, and shattered. The second brain-drained Mantid whirled in a spiral and then shot top-first toward the ground. *CRASH!* The drone's body smashed apart upon impact. The third flying attacker landed on top of the second in a lifeless heap.

"I'd better get out of here," Josh whispered, half in awe. He returned his weapon to the satchel. Then, turning his back to the hive, he ran faster than he'd ever run before. The young Turok ran as swiftly as the wind, powered by the chaps he wore on his muscular legs. Seconds later he was back with Barry and Alison.

"W-We saw what happened," Barry sputtered. "They attacked you for no reason."

"Nice duds, Bro," Alison said as she checked out her brother's new outfit. "How about yanking a fresh set of threads out of that bag for me?"

"I don't think I have anything in your size," Josh quipped as he led his sister and his best friend back into the woods. "If the rest of those Mantids attack, we're doomed. Come on. Let's head for those cliffs on the other side of the forest." The weary travelers dashed into the foliage without so much as a backward glance at the buzzing alien hive.

# Chapter 6

"This isn't The Lost Land, it's a giant loony bin," Alison said as she followed the trail her brother blazed through the forest. "All we do is pinball from one dangerous place to another. First we're attacked by some huge Loch Ness-type Dinosoid. Then a flying leftover from the prehistoric age swoops down on us. Next, alien bugs use my bro for target practice." She glanced over her shoulder at Barry, who was behind her. "Doesn't any of this bother you, Einstein?"

Barry shrugged his bony shoulders. "What good does it do to worry?" he replied. "We got here when some type of dimensional portal opened. There must be a way to open a portal again to get back through and go home. We just don't know where the portals are or how to open them. Maybe Josh will eventually discover something in his satchel that can help us locate one of them. We'll have to be patient and try to stay alive until he does."

Alison froze in her tracks. Barry, who wasn't really watching where he was going, bumped into her.

"Be patient and stay alive, huh?" Alison grumbled. "Gee, that sounds so simple when you put it like that. We have a chance . . . if we can just . . . stay alive!" She put her nose in Barry's face. "Listen, Genius," she snapped. "Put that big brain of yours to work and try to figure out an escape plan or something. I want to get home in time for the Marilyn Manson concert, remember?"

"Yo! Back off, Alison," Barry snapped, feeling annoyed at this verbal assault. "I like you and everything, and you're my best friend's sister, but now you're in my face. So chill out. We're doing the best we can."

He pushed past her and continued down the trail.

Alison's eyes opened wide in amazement. Barry had never ever spoken to her like that before. Sure, he liked to kid around, but she had never seen him show his anger before. This new side of him was most definitely interesting.

Barry halted. "Well?" he yelled to Alison. "Are you coming or not?"

Alison smiled and nodded. Dodging all these Dinosoids in The Lost Land was beginning to make Barry Hackowitz stand up for himself. She liked the change. "I'm with you," she said. Then she fell into step behind the two boys.

"We're getting closer to the cliffs," Josh called out from his lead position. "I can see a narrow pass ahead. We're coming to a clump of boulders. We'll stop there to rest."

Barry sighed in an exhausted fashion. "Good," he replied. "I'm beat."

The threesome exited the forest and made for a pile of huge brown and gray boulders. Some of the boulders were the size of dump trucks back on Earth. As they neared one strangely shaped rock, it began to move slightly. They were weary travelers too tired to notice.

"I'm going to stretch out on this boulder and catch some rays," Alison said.

"Tanning is dangerous," Barry warned as he followed close behind. "It can be hazardous to your health."

"Everything in Galyanna is hazardous to my health," Alison replied.

"Good point," conceded Barry. "Maybe this whole place needs some kind of a giant Surgeon General's warning."

Josh laughed and sat down on a small rock the size of a desk.

Alison slowly stepped closer and closer to the odd boulder. Without warning a huge turtlelike head shot out of the front of the rock. This was not a big stone, but a huge flesh-eating snapping turtle. The slow-moving beast would snap up any living creature that ventured too close to its monstrous jaws.

Barry noticed the turtle's head first. "Look out!" he yelled as he dove forward and shoved Alison out of harm's way.

"Eek!" shrieked Alison. She fell roughly to the ground as the creature's jaws snapped at the thin air where she had been standing.

Josh leaped to his feet and ran to his sister's side.

Meanwhile, Barry, who'd tumbled to the ground when he'd shoved Alison to safety, became the turtle's next target. "Yeow!" Barry yelled as he crouched low and back-pedaled away from the creature's snapping jaws. Barry scooted over to Alison and Josh.

"Y-You saved my life," she said as she got to her feet.

"Forget it," Barry answered. "Next time you can save mine."

The giant snapping turtle was on the move.

"You two, get in there," ordered Josh, pointing to a narrow crevice between two large boulders. "I'll try to distract it."

Barry and Alison squeezed into the narrow crack. The turtle lumbered toward its prey, then tried to poke its head into the crevice. The beast's head was too large.

"Anytime, Josh!" yelled Alison. "We're ready for that distraction!"

"Working on it," replied Josh as he reached into the Light Burden and pulled out a heavy pistol. He fired point-blank at the creature confronting his companions.

*POW! POW! BLAM! BLAM! KA-POW!* Bullets struck the turtle's shell and were harmlessly deflected. Josh kept firing. Bullet after bullet bounced off of the monster's thick protective plating. The creature appeared invincible. Josh couldn't harm it, or turn its attention away from his cornered companions.

"Bullets are completely useless," Josh yelled to Barry. "Do you have any suggestions?"

"Well, it's a turtle, right?" Barry shouted back as he and Alison clung to each other inside the crevice. "Turtles are helpless on their backs. Do you have anything in your satchel powerful enough to flip it over?"

"I don't know," Josh answered, candidly. He put down the heavy pistol. The young Turok opened the Light Burden and concentrated intensely as he dug deep into his interdimensional arsenal. Out came a grenade launcher.

"I think I've found something that may do the trick!" Josh yelled. "Hunker down and protect yourselves. There's going to be one mighty big explosion."

Josh lifted the grenade launcher. He waited until he was sure Alison and Barry were out of the line of fire. Carefully, he aimed at the rear of the giant turtlelike monster. His finger curled around the trigger, and then jerked.

*BLAM! WHIZZZ!* The grenade was launched. It landed in the perfect position to do the most harm to the monster without injuring Barry and Alison.

*KA-BLAM!* The grenade exploded with such force that the turtle beast was violently hurled up into the air. Its legs thrashed wildly and it roared in rage as it flipped over.

78

*WHUMP!* The creature came down hard on its thick shell, exposing its soft underbelly to attack.

There was still no way Barry and Alison could get past the creature's jaws, even though it was upside down. Clutching the heavy pistol in his right hand, Turok bounded from rock to boulder, gaining a height advantage above the monster.

He leaped courageously onto the monster's underside, firing his pistol at its heart as he landed. *BANG! POW! POW! POW!* The bullets ripped into the turtle's flesh and tore into its massive heart. The beast kicked spasmodically, grunted loudly, and died belly up in the sun.

"It's safe to come out now," Josh called down to his sister and friend. "The thing is dead."

Slowly, Alison and Barry crept out of the crack between the stones. They held each other tightly and cringed in terror as they slipped past the monster's limp head.

"Have I said before that I don't like it here?" commented Alison as they resumed their march to nowhere.

"I guess it's not so bad, if you've got a Turok with you," quipped Barry. "We'll have to remember to include that tip when we write the travel guide for this place."

Josh glanced at the sun which was setting behind the mountains above them. "We need to find a good place to camp for the night," he said. "It's almost dusk."

"Good," said Alison. "I'm beat."

Josh led the way down the rocky pass. As the sun sank lower in the sky he began to search for a campsite that might provide them with some protection from attack.

"Look!" Barry called as they rounded a bend. He stopped and pointed at a large opening in solid rock just ahead. When they got closer they discovered it was a cave. The entrance was about ten feet high. "Why don't we camp in there."

"Beggars can't be choosers," Josh admitted. "Let's check it out."

"Check it out?" Alison repeated. "I say let's check in. It's getting dark and I can't walk another step. I need sleep."

Josh glanced at Barry. Barry shrugged his shoulders. "There's a lot of dry wood lying around," he said. "If we stop now we can collect enough to make a good-sized fire."

"Don't tell me you brought along matches?" Alison remarked.

Barry turned and grinned. "Eagle Scout

Hackowitz doesn't need matches to start a fire," he announced proudly. "Just a couple of sticks and years of intensive training."

Alison nodded. She began to collect dried-up twigs and branches. "I'm impressed," she admitted. "Now if you can just produce some hot dogs and marshmallows, we can all gather around the fire and sing camp songs."

Josh laughed. He began to collect sticks and branches. The three companions carried the kindling over to the mouth of the cave. They dropped the wood in a pile and stood peering into the dark hole in the cliff. It was still light enough to see outside, but the cavern was pitch-black inside.

"I'll nose around a little inside while you get a fire going," Josh said to Barry. Josh was still carrying the heavy pistol he'd used to dispel the giant snapping turtle. He cocked the weapon and boldly ventured into the bleak bowels of The Lost Land.

Alison and Barry watched as Josh was swallowed up by the blackness. One minute he was visible and the next he was completely out of sight.

"Help me pile up the wood," Barry said to Alison. She nodded. Together they turned their attention to the task of starting a fire.

Inside the cave, Josh slowly prodded deeper into the darkness. His eyes adjusted somewhat to the lack of light, but visibility was still poor at best. Step by step, he explored as much of the cave as he dared. About a hundred yards into the large cavern it split into two smaller tunnels. The tunnels went in opposite directions and bore down deep beneath the surface. Josh stopped. *There's no sense in going further,* he thought. *The cave seems safe enough.* He craned his neck to look up at the ceiling. It was totally black. He couldn't see the roof.

Josh turned and headed back toward the entrance. He didn't realize his every move was being watched from above. Clinging to the roof of the unlit cavern was a legion of Galyanna's deadliest creatures.

As he neared the entrance to the cavern, Josh saw the bonfire blazing at the mouth of the cave. "Once a scout, always a scout," he muttered, thinking of Barry. The blazing bonfire illuminated the front portion of the cavern. Josh got his first really good look at the natural rock formation. Although the cave's mouth was only about ten feet high, the cavern itself was immense. The roof soared thirty or forty feet above him.

"This is some place, isn't it?" Barry said as

Josh walked up. "It's huge. I couldn't believe how big it was when I got the fire going. Maybe we can put up a basket and shoot some hoops." Barry paused. "Did you see anything back there?"

Josh shook his head. "It seems clear," he answered. "I really can't be sure, though. It was pretty dark." He looked at his sister, who was cuddled up near the roaring fire. "I thought you'd be roasting marshmallows by now," he teased. Alison glared at her brother. If looks could kill, her eyes would have fired tracer bullets.

"She's really hungry," Barry whispered to Josh. Josh nodded. He felt bad about teasing her. Alison could be a real pain, but they'd been through a lot together, growing up with a father who drank, then disappeared one day, and a mother who left when she just couldn't take it anymore, leaving her oldest daughter to raise the two younger siblings. For all their teasing and competition, Josh and Alison cared deeply for each other and were fiercely loyal to one another and their older sister.

Not to mention what the three companions had been through in the time since they arrived in Galyanna. Josh looked at his sister whose eyes were starting to close.

"Maybe we'll be able to find something to eat tomorrow," Josh said softly to Alison.

Alison smiled faintly.

"What we all need now is some rest," Josh said. "You guys sleep. I'll stand guard for two hours. Then I'll wake up Barry."

"Don't forget to wake me for guard duty when your shift is done," Alison said to Barry.

"Don't worry about it," Barry answered. "I'll set the clock radio for The Lost Land— alternative rock station, 'WGAL, where Galyanna rocks!' That'll wake you up."

Barry stretched out near the fire and soon drifted off into an uneasy sleep. Josh walked deeper into the cave and sat down. He took up a guard position at the edge of the shadows and peered past the fire toward the mouth of the cave. From that position he could keep tabs on anything approaching their campsite from the front of the cavern or from the back. He placed the heavy pistol in his lap, glanced at his watch, and settled in for his two-hour shift of guard duty.

All was peaceful, yet Josh felt uneasy. He had the strange sensation that he was being watched. At the end of an uneventful two hours, a weary Joshua Fireseed shook his friend Barry Hackowitz awake.

"H-Huh? Don't eat me!" Barry babbled as he opened his eyes. "Oh," he gasped. "Sorry. I guess I was dreaming about some of the friends we've made since we arrived here."

Josh smiled. "It's your turn to stand guard." He handed Barry the heavy pistol. Barry sat up and took the gun. It looked out of place in his inexperienced hands. Barry yawned and walked over to the place where Josh had stood guard. It was at the very curtain of light that separated the campfire from the dark shadows at the rear of the cave.

"Sleep tight," Barry said as Josh lay down in the dirt.

"I will," Josh replied. "I'm so exhausted, a herd of thundering Dinosoids couldn't keep me awake." He shut his eyes and fell fast asleep.

Three hours later, Alison stirred from a restless sleep. She rubbed her eyes and sat up. She looked over to where Barry should have been standing guard. Alison blinked her eyes. Barry was gone! He was nowhere in sight.

"Where did he wander off to?" Alison grumbled. "He never woke me up." She looked at her brother snoozing peacefully near the fire. She was about to wake him, then changed her mind.

85

Josh needed all the sleep he could get. This Turok business was hard work.

"If Barry is goofing off, I'll give him a queen-sized piece of my mind," she vowed. Alison quietly walked over to where Barry should have been. "Barry?" she whispered. She looked deep into the shadows at the rear of the cave. "Barry Hackowitz, quit playing games," she called angrily. Alison moved deeper into the blackness.

Minutes later, Alison's shriek of terror and alarm jarred her brother Josh right out of a peaceful dream. In his dream he'd just smacked a grand-slam home run to win the World Series for the Yankees. The scream acted like a slap in his face. It cleared his head instantly and prodded him into action. He jumped to his feet.

"Alison? Barry?" Josh shouted as his eyes scanned the cavern for signs of his two companions.

"EEEK!" Josh homed in on the sound of Alison screaming. He turned and ran deep into the dark portion of the cavern. His eyes quickly adjusted to the lack of light. Twenty-five yards into the shadows he spied his sister. Alison was backing up toward the wall of the cavern as a huge adult cave spider slowly inched toward her. The gigantic black arachnid was twice the size of a newborn colt. Its mouth was open and razor-sharp four-inch fangs protruded from its jaws.

When the spider saw Turok it turned and hissed loudly. The monster halted and spit a glob of smelly poisonous venom at Josh, who hit the dirt just in time to avoid having the poison splattered in his face.

"Help me, Josh!" Alison shrieked. "You know I hate spiders!" Josh did a forward roll while reaching into the Light Burden as he tumbled. He rolled to his feet and came up holding a shotgun. Without a second's hesitation he cocked the weapon and fired.

*KA-BLAM!* The shotgun blast savagely ripped into the cave spider's body, reducing it to a bloody pile of disconnected arachnid parts. The remains were no longer recognizable as anything that had once been a big, ugly spider.

"Wait by the fire," he ordered. "I'm going to find Barry." Obediently, Alison stumbled off toward the light. Josh turned and moved cautiously into the darkness.

Suddenly, he halted. His eyes rolled upward. He jumped back and raised the barrel of the shotgun. Dangling from a silky thread directly above his head was another huge cave spider. Josh aimed

87

and fired. *KA-BOOM!* The spider's body was blasted apart. Bloody spider legs and body parts rained down on the cave floor as Josh dashed forward.

Finally, he neared the area where the cavern split into two tunnels. The passage was blocked by a huge sticky web constructed by the spiders. Stuck in the center of the web was Barry. He was secured in spread eagle fashion.

"Go back, Josh!" Barry hollered as he struggled uselessly to free himself. "It's a trap. You're being lured into a trap."

"Keep still, " Josh shouted. "I'll have you out of there in a second." He stepped forward. From out of the shadows to Josh's left, a spider spit a glob of poisonous venom. Instinctively, Josh ducked. The venom spitball missed and splattered on the far wall.

Josh whirled on his heels to level the shotgun at the spider, which was now charging toward him. *BLAM!* The shot blast exploded in the spider's face, killing it instantly. A noise to the right alerted Josh to a new threat. He spun to the right and fired. *KA-BOOM!* Another cave spider was reduced to a blood-soaked pile of spider parts.

Fireseed spun around to look for more attackers. For the moment, there were none.

He lowered the smoking shotgun. Reaching into the Light Burden, he pulled out a large knife that had a sharp curved blade and a jewel-encrusted handle. He lifted the gleaming blade and sliced through the strands of spider webbing, freeing his friend.

"Thanks, Bud," Barry said as he rubbed his raw and sore wrists. "I thought I was a spider snack for sure. I heard a noise and came in to investigate. I guess by the time those suckers attacked me I was too far in for you to hear my screams for help."

"What about my pistol?" Josh asked.

"I had it with me, but they startled me and I dropped it," replied Barry. "There it is." Barry picked the Turok weapon off the cave floor and handed it back to Josh.

Josh stared at the tunnels behind the massive web. "There may be more of those monsters lurking in those holes," he said. "Let's get back to the campfire. These things don't seem to like the light. We should be safe if we stay near the fire until morning."

Barry nodded. Together they started for the mouth of the cave. "I'm just glad we piled up plenty of firewood," Barry said. "The only thing more scary than Galyanna during the day is Galyanna at night."

# Chapter 7

Alison, Barry and Josh spent the rest of the night sitting wide awake near the blazing fire. They were all too nervous to sleep. One of them was constantly turning around to survey the surrounding area. Every so often Alison muttered the word, 'spiders!' and shuddered violently. Dawn didn't come quickly enough to suit them.

When the sun finally rose, the threesome prepared to abandon their camp. "I wish we knew where we were going," Alison commented as they stood outside the mouth of the cave.

"What we need is a road map of Galyanna," Barry proposed, half-jokingly.

Josh eyed Barry in a scolding way. "No kidding," Josh stated. "And just where do you expect to get a map?"

Barry and Alison exchanged glances. Together they turned and stared at the Light Burden slung over Josh's shoulder. Josh shrugged. "Hey! It's worth a try," he admitted. He stuck his hand into the satchel and amazingly, pulled out a crude map of The Lost Land. "Well, how about that?" Josh exclaimed. He unfolded the map and began to study it. Josh located the jungles they'd tramped through earlier and the haggard cliffs where they were now. "If we follow this pass we'll end up at some kind of village," he told the others.

"Great," Alison said, her spirits rising for the first time. "Maybe someone there will know how we can get out of here."

"Yeah, maybe we'll finally meet someone who doesn't want us for dinner," added Barry. Then he eyed the Light Burden with a silly smirk on his face.

"What's with you?" Josh asked him.

Barry pointed at the pouch. "It seems that whatever you wish for comes out of that bag," he said.

"So?" Josh interjected.

Barry eagerly rubbed the palms of his

91

hands together. "I was just thinking," he said as his eyebrows rose. "What I really could use right now is a blind date with Jewel." He grinned from ear to ear. "Do you think you could pull her out of your magic bag of tricks?"

Josh glanced at Alison. She rolled her eyes contemptuously. Josh jabbed his hand into the pouch and quickly pulled out a fistfull of empty air.

"Sorry, Bachelor Number One," Josh said as he showed Barry his bare palm. "No Jewel. No date. No instant romance."

Alison laughed out loud. "I guess that magic bag doesn't work for everything," she cackled.

Barry just scowled, slightly embarrassed.

"Let's get going," Josh ordered. "That village is still a long hike away."

It was near noon when they exited the pass and entered a small, lush valley. Much to their astonishment and delight, at the entrance to the valley they stumbled upon a treasure in the form of a large apple tree. The towering tree had many leafy branches, all of which were laden with ripe, succulent fruit.

"We hit the jackpot!" Alison cried happily when she spotted the tree. "I'm so hungry I could eat all those apples."

"They do look plump and tasty," Barry admitted. He licked his lips in anticipation of their first meal since they'd arrived in Galyanna.

The threesome started toward the trunk of the tree. Suddenly the tree began to shake violently. Apples snapped from their stems and dropped to the ground below the tree. The shaking continued and a torrent of fruit fell from the tree limbs.

"There's something in the tree," Barry said to his friends. "And whatever it is, it's big and it's strong. I'm guessing *it* likes apples, too."

The tree shook and shook until the ground below was littered with plenty of fruit. The shaking stopped. The leaves in the middle of the tree rustled. The thing in the tree was climbing down to enjoy a feast of fruit.

Out of the branches dropped a monstrous apelike creature. It had long, hairy legs and huge, powerful arms. The brutish beast seemed to have humanoid features but appeared somewhat slow-witted. When it hit the dirt it didn't notice the three strangers standing nearby. Calmly, it began to scoop up apples and rapidly cram them into its mouth, one after another.

"What do you think that is?" Barry

whispered. Josh shook his head. "I don't have a clue. Maybe it's some kind of missing link."

"Whatever it is, it's not armed," Josh noticed. "Maybe it's harmless."

"Right," Alison said. "And it doesn't rain during a monsoon." Josh shot his sister an icy look.

At that moment the creature, known in Galyanna as a War Club, spotted the humans. All thoughts of the beast being peaceful and harmless quickly vanished. It growled angrily and ran toward a nearby pile of rocks. It hefted a huge boulder and easily raised it over its head. The War Club launched its stone projectile in the direction of Josh, Alison, and Barry.

"Look out!" Josh yelled as they scattered. The boulder landed in the spot where they'd just been standing, crashing to the ground with a loud thud.

The beast snarled in a rage. It bared its teeth and prepared to charge.

"Shoot it!" Alison screamed.

"No," Josh refused. "I don't think that will be necessary."

"Well, do something," begged Barry frantically. "That thing's not charging over here to shake our hands."

"More than likely he'll rip our arms off and beat us over our heads with them," Alison predicted.

"Relax," called Josh as he dashed forward to meet the charge of the War Club head-on. "It's Fireseed the slugger to the rescue."

"Huh?" said Alison and Barry at the same time.

Josh pulled a baseball bat out of the Light Burden as he raced toward the apelike brute. Just before they smacked into each other, Josh jumped high into the air and somersaulted over the beast's head. He landed on his feet behind the creature and grasped his bat with two hands.

The War Club skidded to a stop and tried to turn.

"It's a hit-and-run play," Josh yelled, jumping in front of the beast. He whacked it across the back of its calves. The creature tumbled to the ground.

Getting up, the War Club growled as Josh assumed a batting stance. The beast swung a massive fist in Josh's direction. "Strike one," Josh yelled as he ducked. At the same time he jabbed the end of his bat into the beast's belly. The force of the jab caused the War Club to double over.

Josh whirled behind the beast.

"Bottom of the fifth," he hollered. He swung the bat and whacked the brute across its bottom. The War Club howled in pain. It grabbed its posterior and raced off into the woods leaving the apple tree unattended.

Josh leaned on his bat. "I've just won the batting title of Galyanna," Josh announced. Barry and Alison applauded appreciatively. "Now let's enjoy the fruits of my victory," Josh invited. He waved his arm at the apples lying beneath the tree.

"Gee," Alison said as she scrambled toward the fruit. "I sure hope an apple a day keeps the monsters away. I plan to eat at least a dozen."

"Save some for me," Barry called. Then turning to Josh he added, "How did you know that big ape wouldn't try to rip us to pieces?"

"Somehow I could tell that he was just defending the apples," replied Josh. "Something told me not to kill him. Not to ever kill unless it was absolutely necessary."

"Turok's intuition, huh?" Barry said.

Josh just shrugged as the three of them sat down in the shade of the apple tree and began to eat. The fruit wasn't particularly sweet or juicy, but they were the best apples the trio had ever tasted.

When their appetites were satisfied, they leaned back against the trunk of the apple tree. *Burp!* Barry's eyes opened wide in embarrassment. "Excuse me," he apologized. "I think gobbling down all that fruit gave me gas."

"Belching in public is probably considered good manners in Galyanna," Alison teased. "I'm sure Dinosoids don't care which fork they use to pluck prey out of the jungle."

Suddenly Josh rose to a sitting position. He twisted around to look in one direction and then another. "Speaking of Dinosoids," he stated, "listen: do you hear that?"

Alison and Barry sat up and listened. There was a faint sound like distant thunder echoing through the valley. The noise got louder and louder.

Alison looked up at the sky. It was clear. There wasn't a storm cloud in sight.

"Quick!" Josh urged. "Take cover!" Josh, Barry, and Alison scrambled over to the cluster of rocks where the War Club had taken the boulder. They ducked down and hid. From their hiding place they watched and waited. The thunderous footsteps got louder and louder and louder.

Suddenly, a dozen Dinosoid descendants of the savage Tyrannosaurus Rex came crashing out of the foliage. The huge Dinosoids, called Endtrails, were powerfully built, bloodthirsty bipeds who were elite members of the Dinosoid Army. Each one of the massive monsters was equipped with an ion gauntlet that it wore on one of its tiny arms. The ion gauntlet could fire explosive energy charges. The Endtrails roared savagely as they thundered past the hidden threesome.

"They sure were in a big hurry," Alison said when the T-Rex Dinosoids had passed.

"Maybe they were late for the all-you-can-eat buffet at Café Galyanna," quipped Barry.

"I wonder what those things were on their hands?" Josh asked. "They looked like some type of weapon."

"I'm just glad they didn't see us," Alison said. She shook her head. "Can you imagine what it would be like to have to fight with something that big?"

Josh looked at the trail of crushed foliage and trampled ground the Endtrails had left in their wake. He noted the direction in which they were heading. Then he pulled out the map he had stuffed into his pants pocket. He unfolded the map and checked it over. His facial expression soured.

"What is it, Josh?" Alison inquired. "What's wrong?"

"Those Dinosoids seem to be headed for the same village that we are," he announced in a concerned tone. "I only hope that when we get there, there is someone left alive to talk to!"

Shock registered on Alison's face. Barry gulped. Josh stuffed the map in his pocket. "I don't know what good it will do, but we've got to try to help whoever lives in that village. Let's go!"

Josh ran off in hot pursuit of the monsters that had just passed. Alison and Barry did their best to keep up with him. Before long, they heard the sound of energy blasts and massive explosions. As they came closer to the village, they heard savage growls and shrieks of terror. The threesome exchanged glances as the screams blended into one long, anguished wail of torment.

# Chapter 8

Joshua Fireseed emerged from out of the foliage at the edge of the small village and came face to face with a startling scene of brutal devastation.

The giant T-Rex Dinosoids were ravaging what seemed to be a peaceful community of harmless fruit gatherers. Wicker baskets filled with various kinds of fruits were stored outside of simple huts made of bamboo poles and large ferns and palm leaves. The huts were clustered in rings around a strange glowing pole in the very center of the village. The pole seemed to pulsate with power.

The inhabitants of the village were tiny

aliens dressed in animal pelts and skirts of leaves. Their skin was the color of emerald-green moss. They stood three or four feet tall at full height and had one large eye in the center of their foreheads. Even though they were armed with short spears, daggers, and tiny crossbows, it was obvious they were not a warlike tribe. On each hand they had six fingers. The extra finger was an additional thumb.

The six-fingered fruit gatherers were being methodically slaughtered as they tried in vain to protect their village from the Endtrails. Josh saw an adult male launch a spear into the thick hide of a T-Rex attacker. The Dinosoid flicked the spear point out of its body and leaned down toward its attacker. The Endtrail snapped up the tiny defender in its massive jaws and crunched the green body between its razor sharp teeth. Green blood streamed out of the monster's mouth as tiny arms and legs fell to the ground.

Another Dinosoid raider aimed its ion wrist gauntlet at a row of flimsy huts. *ZAP! ZAP! BOOM! KA-BLAM!* Powerful energy charges flew from the gauntlet, exploding the buildings and reducing them to piles of smoldering sticks and burning branches.

Everywhere he looked, Josh saw throngs of frantic villagers fleeing for their lives before the onslaught of the marauding monsters. He cringed in shock as giant Endtrails stomped around, purposely stepping on helpless villagers. Their piercing cries of anguish echoed in his ears.

Some adult villagers courageously fought to protect their homes and families but to no avail. Defenders were ripped apart by flashing claws and jaws or blasted to smithereens by powerful energy charges. The ground ran green with the emerald blood of the peaceful mossy aliens.

"I've got to help them," Josh said angrily as he gritted his teeth and reached into the Light Burden.

"No, Josh," begged Alison. "The Dinosoids are too big and there are too many of them. You'll only get yourself killed." She tried to hold her brother in check.

"That's a risk I'll have to take," Josh said as he broke free of her grasp. Out of the Light Burden came Turok's awesome Firestorm Cannon. Clutching the deadly weapon in his hands, Joshua Fireseed raced into the murderous fray. He quickly came face-to-face with a T-Rex Dinosoid towering over a young green female clutching a screaming child in her arms. The woman shrieked as the Dinosoid raised its gigantic foot to crush the life out of her and her baby.

"Oh no you don't!" Josh yelled as he raced forward. He lifted the Firestorm Cannon and pulled the trigger. *BRAT-A-TAT-TAT!* A hail of bullets tore into the body and head of the powerful Endtrail. The lethal rain of lead ripped into the reptilian monster's hide. In seconds, the great beast was a mass of lifeless pulp.

"Quick!" Josh said as he helped up the mother and child. "Run for the forest!"

"Over here!" called Alison, waving to the female villager.

"Thank you," the mother sobbed as she looked at Josh. With her baby in her arms she dashed off toward where Alison and Barry were hiding.

Josh ran in the other direction. He closed in on another Dinosoid trooper. *ZAP! BOOM!* The Dinosoid used its ion gauntlet to explode another hut. Debris flew into the air along with the lifeless body parts of three mutilated villagers.

"How about shooting at someone who can shoot back!" Josh roared as he squeezed the trigger of the Firestorm Cannon. A hailstorm of red-hot tracer bullets buzzed into the hide of the monster like a swarm of deadly lead bees. The T-Rex snarled in pain and dropped to the ground. Josh hurled the dying Dinasoid by its twitching tail and continued toward the center of the village.

As he ran, Josh passed hysterical villagers fleeing in panic. At the center of the village he saw an old man cowering at the base of the glowing pole. Two Dinosoids were approaching the old man from opposite directions. Josh aimed the Firestorm Cannon at the closest T-Rex.

"Get down," he yelled to the small green elder. Josh squeezed the firing mechanism. The gun erupted in a burst of lethal fire. Non stop bullets pelted the Dinosoids, perforating its body with hundreds of holes. The great creature crashed to the ground.

While Josh busied himself with one Endtrail, another one grabbed the glowing pole, yanked it out of its mooring in the ground, and prepared to flee. Grasping the pulsating pole tightly, the Dinosoid trooper turned tail and ran. The attack stopped as quickly as it had begun. The remaining Dinosoids quickly joined in the hasty retreat.

"No! No!" lamented the village elder.

"Stop them! Don't let them get away. Stop them with your weapon," he begged Josh.

Josh shook his head. "They're leaving," he answered. "They've had enough." He patted the hot barrel of his Firestorm Cannon. "I guess I taught them a thing or two." He glanced around. Everywhere he looked, bodies and wreckage were strewn around on the ground. Villagers were crying over wounded or dead family members. Not a hut in the village was left standing. "I just wish I could have gotten here sooner," he sighed.

The elder shook his head sadly. "The Energy Totem," he rasped. "Without it we cannot survive. All is lost. All is lost," he repeated.

"I don't understand," Josh said. "You've suffered terrible casualties and your village is destroyed, but you can rebuild."

"Without our only source of power, the soil will dry up and fail to sustain our orchards," the elder said. "There will be no trees and no fruit. We have no other way to get the water to our crops in this dry environment. Our lush valley will turn into a desolate horrible place."

Slowly the surviving villagers began to creep out of hiding. Gradually they assembled at the center of the village where Josh and the elder stood. Alison and Barry also ventured forward.

"Look!" yelled a man as he pointed at the place where the totem had stood. "The sacred object is gone! The Evil One's troops have stolen it."

"Now we are doomed," wailed a woman. "How can we survive? Where will we go?"

The elder slowly blinked his one eye. He turned to look at what was left of his tribe. "We will go to The Safelands," he told them. "The Council of Voices will know what to do. Yes, there we will be protected for the time being. We will bury our dead and then leave immediately for The Safelands."

The elder started to walk away. Josh put a hand on the old man's shoulder. "I'm sorry about what happened," he apologized, "but we need your help. We came here for some information."

"I sense that there is much about Galyanna you do not understand, young warrior," the elder said. "There is a great new danger in the land. It is said that Primagen has awakened. It was his evil recruits that you fought. He controls them with his telepathic power." He looked at Barry and Alison. "The answers to your questions lie in The Safelands. The Council of Voices resides there and will tell you all. You are welcome to journey with us."

"Council of Voices?" Alison muttered quizzically.

"Safelands?" mumbled Barry in puzzlement.

"Galyanna is a very dangerous place," explained the village elder.

"So we have learned," said Barry.

"Danger lurks around every bend," continued the elder. "Except for The Safelands. As the name implies, it is a place of sanctuary, where all peaceloving beings are welcomed by the Council of Voices."

"What is this Council of Voices you keep referring to?" asked Barry.

The elder turned to face Barry. "Young man, The Council of Voices is the ruling body of The Safelands. They have existed for countless centuries. It is our only hope to survive as a people."

Josh looked the elder in his one eye. "We'll be going with you," he stated. The elder nodded and walked away.

Late that afternoon the three refugees from Earth started their desperate journey to The Safelands with the survivors of the fruit-gathering tribe.

The Emerald Elder was a shrewd leader who knew all the trails and safe camp areas in Galyanna. Following down along the Vermes River, the party of earthlings and villagers evaded several small detachments of Dinosoid troopers, all of whom were moving steadily northward. At night the group spent the dark hours resting in the boughs of tall purple spruce trees.

At daybreak they resumed their trek. After marching at a brisk pace for most of the morning, they reached the Safelands. By this time it was almost noon.

"So this is The Safelands," remarked Barry as the refugee band wandered into the lush, peaceful valley. It was a welcome haven. Located in a remote section of Galyanna, it was protected from The Lost Land's evil inhabitants by the limitless mental power of the Council of Voices. "I expected us to pass through some pearly gates or something. I didn't even hear any trumpets sound." He and the others looked around.

"Now that we're here how do we find this Council of Voices?" asked Josh.

The Emerald Elder stopped and looked at the young Turok. "We do not have to look for the Council of Voices," he said calmly. "We will be contacted."

Barry laughed. "What are they going to

do," he whispered to Alison, "materialize in a puff of smoke?'

Alison giggled. "Maybe they'll appear in a bubble like the Good Witch in *The Wizard of Oz*."

The words were no sooner out of Alison's mouth than a bright sphere of glimmering light appeared before the group. They were all forced to shield their eyes with their hands.

"What is it?" Josh asked. "I-Is it dangerous?"

"There is nothing to fear," a soft, melodious female voice answered. "I am Adon, the Speaker of Forever Light. I speak for the Council of Voices."

Gradually the glow dimmed enough for Josh and the others to uncover their eyes. As the blinding light faded, a tall, beautiful young woman appeared. Her thick braid of long blond hair fell down her back past her waist. She was attired in a brown bodysuit with gold epaulets and circuitry mesh built into the suit. On each sleeve were large forearm plates that served as direct electronic connectors to the Council of Voices.

Boldly, Josh stepped forward. "We're here to see the Council of Voices. Are you one of them?"

Adon shook her lovely head. "No," she replied. "It is my job to channel the telepathic voices of the four members of the Council."

"Why can't we see the members of the Council of Voices?" Josh wanted to know. "No offense, but you don't look much older than I am. How can anyone as young as you help us?"

Adon's full, red lips curled up into a smile. "I appear young, but my appearance and consciousness have been stored in The Safelands Central Computer for almost five hundred years."

Alison whistled in astonishment. "Wow! Five hundred years old and she doesn't have one wrinkle."

"You should look so good when you're five hundred," Barry said to Alison, who elbowed him in the ribs by way of reply.

"My physical presence before you is an image created by the central computer," Adon explained.

"Some kind of a holographic projection," expounded Barry.

Josh nodded. "I still don't understand why the Council of Voices aren't here in person."

"They are much older than my program," Adon answered. "Their bodies are stored in stasis tanks and their minds are linked into one central unit. I am their link with the corporeal world. I am programmed to relay their thoughts and emotions. I give voice to their minds, wisdom, and compassion. They live through me."

Adon turned to the tribal elder. "Take your people to the Grove of Plenty and wait there," she instructed. "I will tend to your concerns later."

The village elder bowed respectfully. Without saying a word he motioned to the remnants of his tribe to follow him.

"Uh, Adon," Barry called out. "These members of the Council of Voices. Are they human?"

"One is human," she responded. "One is Dinosoid. Two are members of other species."

"Let's cut to the chase here," Alison said curtly. "Do you know how we can get out of this dreadful place?"

Josh spun to face his sister. "Put a lid on it, Alison!" he ordered. "This is her home." As he turned, the Light Burden swung out from his body. Adon noticed it for the first time.

"You," she said, pointing a holographic finger at Joshua. "Which Turok

111

are you? Have you come to Galyanna to help the Secondary?"

"Huh?" Josh stammered. He shrugged his shoulders. "Who is the Secondary?"

"The Turok known as Carl Fireseed."

Josh's shoulders slumped. He lowered his head and glanced back at his sister. Alison's chin drooped. She shook her head. Josh looked at Adon. "Carl Fireseed is dead," he told her. "I'm Joshua Fireseed, Carl's nephew."

"So," remarked Adon. "The mantle has been passed." She paused. "The Council of Voices is sorry to learn of the Secondary's death. He was a great and courageous Turok." She stared at Joshua. "We are sure you will be an equally fearless and brave Turok."

"Here we go again," Josh whispered. After all that had already happened in The Lost Land, Joshua still wasn't sure he could handle the job of Protector of Earth.

"We are glad you are here to help us with the dire problem Primagen now presents. If Primagen's evil escape plan is not thwarted, Earth and Galyanna are doomed to utter and complete destruction. He must not be allowed to return to his own universe." Adon then bowed her head in homage to Joshua.

"The Council of Voices welcomes you, Joshua Fireseed, as the new Turok."

Josh inhaled a deep breath. There seemed to be no escaping his destiny. He asked himself glumly, *Just once can't someone ask me if I want to be Turok instead of telling me I'm already stuck with the job?*

# Chapter 9

Adon sensed how weary the three travelers were and arranged for them to rest in a structure that resembled an ancient Greek temple. The inside rooms of the temple were furnished with unusual-looking furniture but designed for maximum comfort. There were antigravity chairs and sofas that floated above the floor without supports. A variety of food and drinks were also provided, and the threesome ate hungrily. After they were rested and well-fed, Adon once again appeared in their midst.

"Greetings, Turok," she said as she materialized before Josh. Josh slid off the softest chair he'd ever sat in and stood before Adon.

"Whoa, I'm not Turok yet," he replied. "I'm sort of a Turok-in-training. I haven't officially accepted the job."

"There is no time for training," Adon stated. "Now is the time for action. First, tell me what you have encountered since you arrived in Galyanna."

Josh quickly recounted the threesome's Lost Land adventures for Adon.

"Primagen has awakened and continues to enlist weak-minded slaves to assist him in his plan," she said when Josh had finished his story.

"His telepathic power is great. That is why the creatures of Galyanna attacked you so fiercely. Primagen knows that if he can destroy the new Turok, his chances for success increase greatly." She pointed at Josh. "The Council of Voices will do everything in their power to assist you, but it is Turok who must defeat Primagen, and Primagen knows this. The ultimate survival or destruction of all worlds depends on you."

"Primagen?" Barry muttered. He jumped off of an antigravity sofa. "Is Primagen a Dinosoid?" Alison asked, joining Barry and her brother.

"Primagen is an alien." Adon explained. "As he journeyed in his Light Ship to discover other worlds, bits and pieces of those universes attached themselves to his ship, ultimately forming the patchwork dimensions that is Galyanna. The Light Ship acted like a great magnet, you might say. That is why Galyanna is home to so many different types of beings.

"By creating Galyanna," Adon continued before her awestruck audience of three, "he became trapped in the Light Ship. For millions of years since, Primagen has drifted in a semiconscious state, not fully awake. Now he has awakened, and his sole purpose is to power up his Light Ship and try to return to his own universe. If he is successful in attempting the journey to his universe, then our universe, including Galyanna and Earth, will be ripped apart."

Josh looked at Adon with confusion. "Isn't it cruel to prevent someone from going home, even it if means our destruction?" asked Josh.

"You don't have to be so bighearted all the time," whispered Barry.

"We believe that Primagen's universe no longer exists," explained Adon. "It was destroyed when our universe began.

116

Therefore, he has no home to return to. We also believe he knows this but is willing to take the slim chance that he can somehow travel through time and get back home before his universe was destroyed."

"What I don't understand," Barry remarked, "is what prevents Primagen from powering up his Light Ship at any time?"

Adon glanced at Barry. "Thousands of years ago, the Council of Voices created twelve totems to hold the energy force Primagen brought with him. Then they scattered the totems throughout The Lost Land. The totems serve two purposes: first, they keep Primagen from attempting his journey home and tearing all of the other universes apart as he leaves; and secondly, the totems are used to power cities and villages like the one you encountered. The totems merely hold the energy. Primagen needs to pull all the energy from the totems in order to start his ship," she told the group.

Alison stroked her chin thoughtfully. "If those Energy Totems keep Primagen under wraps, what's the big problem?"

"If the totems are captured, Primagen will be able to harness their power to start up his ship," replied Adon.

Joshua whistled in astonishment.

"Primagen sounds like a tough customer. I bet that's why those Dinosoids attacked the village. They were telepathically controlled by Primagen. He didn't send them to kill the villagers, he sent them to get the Energy Totem. The fruit-gatherers use them as a power source." He shook his head as if to scold himself. "And I let them cart it away."

Adon looked at Joshua. "You are quick to assess the situation, Turok," she told him. "Primagen's mind slaves and allies seek to collect the remaining Energy Totems in order to free their master. They already have two, and a third is now also in danger of being captured."

"Two?" exclaimed Josh, looking up in surprise. "When did they capture the other one?"

"The Fireborns collected it," Adon said. "The Council of Voices sent the Secondary to investigate the incident. That was the last time we saw or heard from the one you call Carl Fireseed."

Anger now flashed in Joshua's eyes. He realized that Primagen had been the indirect cause of his uncle's horrible death. And Primagen was an accomplice to murder. The twisted alien held captive in a prison of its own making at the core of Galyanna was responsible for countless deaths . . . but now, for Joshua Fireseed, it was personal.

"Turok," began Adon, "you must gather and protect the other totems to prevent Primagen's legions from capturing them. It is your responsibility. The fates of Galyanna, Earth, and all of their inhabitants rests on your shoulders and your shoulders alone."

Barry and Alison looked at Josh. His face was a hardened mask of stone. They could tell Adon's comments weighed heavily on his conscience.

"You said a third Energy Totem was in danger of being captured," Josh said. He stared at Adon with cold, icy eyes. "Tell me how to find it."

Adon smiled faintly as if she had known all along exactly what Joshua would say. "The Council of Voices has already prepared a hovercraft to take you to the site," she answered. "You are to use the craft to collect that totem and the others to keep them from being captured by Primagen's evil legions." Adon's eyes seemed to twinkle as she studied the face of the young Turok. She found him appealing and intriguing. He was unlike anyone she'd ever encountered. "You will not travel to the place of danger alone, brave Turok," Adon said.

"The Council of Voices has appointed me to be your guide."

"Hey!" Alison said. She stepped forward and took up a position between Adon and her brother. "What about us?" Alison stared at Adon. She wasn't sure she liked the way Adon was eyeing her handsome and muscular brother. Alison had seen other young women back in Oklahoma look at Josh the same way.

"Yeah," Barry chimed in. "What about us?"

"You may remain here in The Safelands or accompany us on our dangerous journey," Adon responded emotionlessly. "In The Safelands there are many forms of alien life. You would have much to occupy your time. There are things you could learn and do. You would be protected and well-fed. The choice is yours."

Alison sneaked a peek at Barry. "Staying here sounds pretty good," Barry whispered, "but I don't want to desert Josh. He may need us."

"Well, guys?" Josh inquired. "What's your decision?"

Alison glanced at Josh and then at Adon. Adon smiled her all-knowing smile.

"Why should we stay here and miss all of

the fun?" Alison said as she folded her arms across her chest and smirked. "Stay here? No way! We're going with you . . . Turok!"

"Hey! I was planning a vacation anyway," Barry agreed, swallowing hard. "A hovercraft ride through The Lost Land sounds kinda nice. Although I kind of pictured myself in someplace more like, oh, I don't know, Fort Lauderdale, perhaps!"

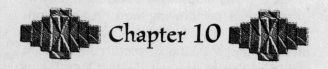

# Chapter 10

The hovercraft containing Josh, Alison, Barry, and the holographic form of Adon silently whisked across the Galyanna landscape. It followed the ancient River of Souls whose path twisted and turned northward. The river had flowed through the wild regions of The Lost Land since the birth of Galyanna millions of years ago.

The poisonous waters of the river ran swift and deep. To sip the lethal liquid meant certain death. Anyone or anything that drank from the deadly River of Souls came to a torturous and painful end. Through the ages the sinister waters had claimed a multitude of unsuspecting victims whose only thought had been to quench their thirst.

"Why is it called the River of Souls?" Alison asked Adon.

Adon, who was piloting the hovercraft, explained. "It is named in memory of the countless number of lives its poisonous waters have claimed."

"If the waters of the River of Souls are so lethal, why are we following it upstream?" Barry wanted to know. "I thought we were going to find an Energy Totem."

Adon kept the hovercraft on course and answered Barry's question at the same time. "Many, many hundreds of years ago, an Energy Totem was erected upstream on the bank of the river," Adon said. "The totem's power cleansed the poisoned water of the river, making it drinkable. In that one secluded bend in the river, the water was miraculously purified." She fell silent for a moment and guided her craft over some treetops. "The water proved to be not only safe to drink, but also a liquid with astonishing healing and growth powers. It gave new vitality to the elderly and infirm. It caused plant life to not only grow at an accelerated rate, but also to yield bounties ten times that of ordinary crops. Because of this, a city sprang up around the totem on the banks of the river."

"The place sounds like a Garden of Eden, a real paradise," Joshua remarked.

Adon nodded. "Yes," she replied. "A paradise. That is a good way to describe it. That is also why it will be difficult to convince the inhabitants of the city that now thrives there to allow us to remove the Energy Totem. Their water would once again be poisoned like the rest of the river."

Joshua sighed. "If they knew that Primagen's Dinosoid allies were traveling north toward their city to steal and destroy their totem, it might convince them of the danger they're in."

"It will be up to you to convince them, Turok," Adon said. "The city lies just ahead."

Joshua Fireseed looked over the bow of the hovercraft. He spied a massive clearing at a wide bend in the river. A large city sat on the banks of the River of Souls. Its buildings were carved out of stone. Beyond the city he could see a great reservoir that was constructed around the totem as both a monument and a place of worship. The purified water of the reservoir was channeled into a complex irrigation system that provided water for cultivated fields in the outlying areas.

The northern border of the city was the River of Souls itself. To the east and west, sheer cliffs created an impassable barrier at the city's edges. To the south, the most vulnerable part of the city, a massive wall was built to protect the inhabitants from attack.

"This sure isn't a simple fruit-gatherer's village," Barry said to Alison as the hover-craft prepared to land. "It's well-fortified."

"That doesn't matter," Josh said. "Even a mighty city is no match for the marauding hordes unleashed by Primagen in his mad quest for the totems." Josh looked around as the hovercraft descended into the square where the Energy Totem was secured. "If the inhabitants of this city refuse to peacefully give up the totem to us so we can protect it until the danger passes, Primagen's evil army will certainly take it by force!"

The hovercraft gently touched down on the ground about thirty yards from the glowing Energy Totem. Quickly a crowd of city dwellers began to congregate. The inhabitants were tall, slender humanoids attired in silky white bodysuits. Their skin was very fair and their shiny hair was almost pure white. They all had flawless complexions and sky-blue eyes. But every adult member of the populace was armed with an energy

125

blaster or rifle. Guards in towers at the south wall were outfitted with portable missile launchers.

"Greetings, Zakus," Adon said as she stepped off the hovercraft. She immediately spoke to an approaching elder wearing an ornate jeweled necklace. "We've been sent to your city by the Council of Voices. Our mission is vital to all of Galyanna."

Zakus bowed in homage to Adon.

"The Speaker of Forever Light and her companions are welcome," the elder said.

Adon turned to look at Josh, Alison, and Barry. "Zakus is the Governor-Elect of this city. He is the decision maker." Adon pointed to Joshua. "This is the new Turok, Joshua Fireseed."

For a brief instant, Zakus's eyes showed a glimmer of shock. "A new Turok?" he repeated softly. "What has become of the Secondary, Carl Fireseed?"

"My uncle was killed by Fireborns," Josh explained. "The Fireborns were sent to attack a village. The villagers were all slaughtered. When my uncle tracked the Fireborns and engaged them in battle, he was mortally wounded."

"My people and I grieve over the loss of the Secondary," Zakus said. Almost on cue, the people gathered in the square. All bowed their heads in homage at the same time.

Slowly, Zakus lifted his head and then addressed Josh. "The Fireborns are deadly enemies," he acknowledged, "but why would they attack a village?"

"They were sent by Primagen," Josh answered sternly and without hesitation. "He has awakened and is telepathically controlling deadly troops all over The Lost Land. Soon Primagen will be sending troops to attack you."

A hush fell over the crowd. One by one the City Dwellers began to whisper to each other. One word, *Primagen*, could be heard as it was repeated again and again.

"We have heard the disturbing reports of Primagen's awakening," Zakus admitted. His concern showed only as a brief flash in his eyes. His face did not indicate the terror he surely felt inside.

"Primagen is a vicious adversary and many denizens of evil serve him. But what would Primagen want of us?"

"That!" Josh said. He stretched out his arm and pointed at the Energy Totem. "The Primagen's troops have already cap-tured two other totems. Primagen will not stop until he has all the totems."

Josh's comments evoked a faint collective gasp of alarm from the City Dwellers. It was the first real emotion any of them had ever expressed.

"The totem is our source of power," Zakus told Josh. "Without it our water will turn foul and putrid. Our crops will die. Our city will crumble and fade from the landscape."

"That is why you can't allow Primagen's troops to capture the totem," Josh advised. "You must give it to us for safekeeping. We'll transport it back to the Safelands where it will be protected from harm until Primagen and his hordes are no longer a threat. Then the totem will be returned to you."

Zakus slowly shook his head. "No," he refused. "We cannot give up the totem."

"No," said a man in the crowd. "Do not surrender the totem."

"It gives us life," a woman said.

"The totem must remain in our possession," another person said.

"I am sorry, Turok," Zakus apologized. "You cannot remove the totem. We do not wish to offend Adon or the Council of Voices, but without the totem this will become a dead city." Zakus pointed at the guards in the towers. He touched the blaster pistol hanging from his belt. "We are not a violent people, but we will fight if we have to. If Primagen's forces come, we will turn them away."

"It's not a matter of *if*," Barry whispered to Alison. "It's more like a matter of *when*."

"You've got to change your mind, Zakus!" Josh insisted. "You're no match for the power of Primagen."

"We shall see," Zakus replied.

"We sure will," Alison cried in alarm. She pointed skyward. "Look!"

In the distant sky four spacecraft could be seen approaching the city. Three of the ships were small, one-pilot fighters. The fighters were bullet-shaped and had long, curved wings. The pointed barrels of blaster cannons protruded from the fronts of the ships.

The three fighters flew in formation around a gigantic, silver mother craft the size of an Earth football field. The mother ship was cigar-shaped. Big propulsion pods connected to long, slender wings that extended out from its sides.

"Skimmer ships," Adon stated. "They are piloted by the Primagen's allies."

"Run for cover," Josh told Barry and Alison.

"We don't have to be told twice," Alison yelled as the crowd in the square began to scatter. The City Dwellers ran toward a large, stone building at the end of the square. They scurried inside, followed by Alison and Barry.

In the sky above the square, the fighters peeled off from the mother ship and prepared to attack. One by one the winged raiders dove down on the city and opened fire.

*WHIZZAP!* An energy blast from the lead fighter hit a manned guard tower. *KA-BOOM!* The tower exploded. The guards manning it were disintegrated.

*WHIZZAP! WHIZZAP! WHIZZAP!* The fighters were pouring lethal fire down on the city. Buildings exploded and guard towers were methodically reduced to rubble. Defenders and innocent bystanders alike were ripped apart by the hail of deadly laser fire. Soon dismembered bodies were strewn all around the square and surrounding areas.

Zakus stood his ground boldly and pulled his blaster from his belt. He fired. *ZAP! ZAP! ZAP!* The fighters easily dodged the destructive charges as the large mother ship took up a position directly above the square.

"They've come for the totem," Josh shouted as he sought cover behind the hovercraft he'd arrived in. Adon was beside him. "Zakus! Tell your people to aim at the mother ship."

Josh reached into the Light Burden, searching for a suitable weapon. He withdrew Turok's Plasma Rifle, the largest rifle in the Turok arsenal. Josh aimed the weapon and fired. Tracer rounds sped skyward toward the belly of the mother ship. Instead of striking, the plasma energy bullets bounced off harmlessly before ever reaching the craft.

The City Dwellers began to unleash a torrent of nonstop fire upon the large, enemy craft. Their energy blasts, missiles and ion bursts never even scratched the surface of the ship. It was as if an invisible barrier protected the ship from attack from below.

"The craft has an energy shield too strong for our weapons to penetrate," Adon quickly explained.

At that moment a compartment in the bottom of the mother ship slowly slid open. Out of the dark opening in the belly of the craft, a tractor beam stretched a finger of light toward the ground. The tractor beam located its target and clamped onto the glowing energy totem. As a savage battle raged around the mother ship, the tractor beam began to pull the Energy Totem out of its mooring.

*KA-BOOM!* A missile, fired from a guard tower, destroyed one of the fighters. Red-hot pieces of smoking metal rained down all around Zakus, Josh, and Adon. Zakus ducked and then looked up in terror as the city's totem was forcibly yanked from the ground.

"Th-They have the totem," he shouted to Josh. "Do something, Turok! Quick! Do something or all will be lost."

Josh clenched his teeth. "What can I do?" he mumbled. "There's no way to disable the mother ship. It's protected by an energy shield from below. . . . Wait!" he cried as an idea occurred to him. "Maybe it can be attacked from above. I bet there's no shield protecting it from above." Josh thought hard. "If I could only get from here to the top of the ship," he said. Josh looked at the Light Burden. He stuck his hand into the satchel. If ever he needed special help, it was now. Josh closed his eyes and concentrated. He pulled out a black, polished opal lens.

"The Folding Eye," Adon said when she saw it. "The mystical key used by Turoks to see invisible spatial portals. The Fold Gate Openings."

"What?" sputtered Joshua as the City's totem slowly rose up into the air. He held up the opal and looked through it with his right eye. To his astonishment, he spied several strange floating apertures—holes of varying sizes. The apertures appeared to be doorways in space. Some of the openings were large enough to drive a truck through. But others were much, much smaller. "What is this folding thing?" he asked.

"Turoks use the Folding Eye to transport themselves from place to place," Adon said. "More than that, I do not know."

Josh reached into his back pocket. Sure enough there was the red bandanna he had brought with him from Earth. He tied the bandanna around his head and affixed the Folding Eye opal lens to it so the jewel was above his right eye.

"Do something! Save the totem!" Zakus implored. "Do something, Turok!"

"I am doing something," Josh assured Zakus. Josh stood up and held the plasma rifle in one hand. With his other hand he reached up and flipped down the Folding Eye. Joshua Fireseed saw a Fold Gate Opening the size of a laundry chute in the center of the plaza.

"I have to believe in myself and the power of Turok," Josh said as he began to run toward the portal. The fighters rained a hailstorm of blaster fire upon him. He raced through the explosions, protected by his breastplate, and dove headfirst into the open portal.

*"ARRRUGH!* Turok yelled as he moved swiftly through darkness. In the distance he saw another Fold Gate Opening, a hole in space. Bright sunlight poured in through the portal. He slid feet first through the portal and emerged directly above the alien mother ship.

*WHUMP!* Turok crash-landed on the top of the hovering spacecraft. "Now the party can start," he announced. He got to his feet and aimed the plasma rifle at the hull of the mother ship.

*BLAM! BLAM! BLAM!* Powerful tracer rounds of plasma energy ripped through the metal, tearing deep into ship's outer skin. The bullets shattered key sensors and instantly ruptured the craft's main stabilizers. The mother ship began to shake, quiver, and wobble.

Quickly, the damaged craft issued an urgent call for assistance. The two remaining fighter ships broke off their attack on the city and came to the aid of their mother ship. In response to the call for help, the fighters focused their attention on the lone intruder clinging precariously to the mother ship's outer hull.

As one fighter turned to commence its attack, Zakus took careful aim with his blaster. He fired. *ZAP!* The energy charge struck the ship and the fighter burst into a whirling ball of fire.

*WHIZZAP! WHIZZAP!* The one remaining fighter opened fire on Turok. As death rays streaked past him, Turok took careful aim and pulled the trigger of the plasma rifle. *BLAM! BLAM! BLAM!* Tracer bullets perforated the hull of the fighter's cockpit. The pilot slumped over his controls as his craft burst into flames, then exploded.

Turok was once again able to direct his attention to the mother ship. The tractor beam was drawing the Energy Totem closer and closer to an opening in the hull. Turok returned the Plasma Rifle to its place within the Light Burden, then reached inside the satchel and pulled out a mine. Turok carefully placed the mine in the gaping gash in the hull created by the Plasma Rifle's tracer rounds.

Turok activated the delayed detonation mechanism. There wasn't much time. The Energy Totem was almost inside the ship. A small green light began to blink on the mine. The countdown began.

Turok flipped down the Folding Eye. Looking around, he spotted a nearby gateway in the sky. "It's time to abandon ship," he shouted. Turok ran and launched himself off the top of the mother ship.

Alison and Barry who had come out of hiding after the last fighter craft exploded, looked up in terror. They saw Josh leap into the air some two hundred feet above their heads. "No!" Alison screamed as she covered her eyes.

"J-Josh!" Barry muttered. He wanted to turn away, but couldn't. To his utter shock, he watched his best friend somersault off of the wobbling alien craft. Josh fell from the ship like a stone, suddenly vanishing into thin air.

A second later, Joshua Fireseed tumbled out of another portal and landed in the dirt at the feet of his concerned companions. At that same instant, the mine he'd planted on the mother craft exploded. *KA-BLAM!* A massive shock wave rocked the city. The mother ship vibrated violently as thick black smoke began to billow out of the gaping hole blasted by the mine. The tractor beam failed and the Energy Totem plummeted to the ground. It landed with a thud in the middle of the soft dirt of the square, undamaged.

"You did it, Turok!" Zakus said as he rushed up to Josh. "You saved the totem."

"But the mother ship is getting away," Barry said. He pointed at the disabled craft, which was slowly retreating. The ship wobbled and belched fire and smoke as it limped back to where it had come from.

"Let it go," said Josh, glancing at the energy totem. "We got what we came for. There's been enough destruction for one day. I won't kill unless it's a matter of life or death."

"That will change the more time you spend in The Lost Land," said Adon. "Either you'll change or I'll be talking to a new Turok very soon."

City Dwellers began to flow into the plaza. "You were right, Turok," Zakus said to Josh. "Take the totem. It must be removed from the city for safekeeping."

"You've made a wise decision, Zakus," Adon said.

Zakus led a group of his people over to the glowing pole. They prepared to load it onto the hovercraft.

"How did you do that little disappearing trick?" Alison asked her brother.

"Yeah," Barry also wanted to know. "You went from one place to another in the blink of an eye. You could make big bucks back on Earth as 'The Amazing Fireseed, escape artist extraordinaire.'"

"I used this," Josh explained as he pointed out the Folding Eye which was attached to his bandanna. "It allows me to see invisible portals."

"Hey!" Barry exclaimed. "Maybe you can locate a portal that will take us home to Earth."

Alison stared at her brother. "Is that possible?" she asked hopefully.

"It should work in theory," said Barry. "Then again, that's what they said about *Windows 95*."

Josh shrugged. "I don't know," he admitted. "I guess it's possible. But first I'm going to have to get a handle on using this Folding Eye gizmo. It worked the way I wanted it to this time, but I was lucky. I also didn't go very far. If we try to get home now, who knows where we might end up?"

"Humph!" Alison grunted. "What place could be worse than this?" She and Barry turned and walked over to the hovercraft.

Joshua looked at Adon. "Looks like that's one Energy Totem for the Good Guys," he said proudly.

Adon nodded. "Now we must get the next

totem," she said. "Doing that might not prove to be as easy as this was."

"Easy!" raged Josh in disbelief. "You call what we just went through . . . easy?"

Adon nodded. "Yes," she said. "For now we must obtain the totem located in the Campaigner's Arena. That will prove to be a great challenge . . . even for the Mighty Turok."

# Chapter 11

The hovercraft containing the rescued totem skimmed over rocky, burning, gaseous terrain. Volcanoes belched forth flames and billows of smoke and ash. "The Campaigner's Arena is located slightly inland from the Vermes River," Adon told the other occupants of the craft. Joshua Fireseed, the reigning Turok, had remained silent and deep in thought since the foursome had left Zakus's city. The words Adon had spoken after Primagen's forces had limped off in defeat, continued to haunt him.

"I won't kill unless it's a matter of life or death," Joshua had said.

"That will change," Adon had vowed, "or I'll be talking to a new Turok very soon."

"A new Turok?" Josh mumbled to himself absentmindedly. "That would suit me fine."

"So," said Adon as she looked at the young hero who had saved Zakus's city and rescued the Energy Totem. "Brave Turok speaks at last. And he awakens from his trance just in time. Soon we will reach the Campaigner's Arena."

"Back off, Adon," Alison commanded. "Leave Josh alone. My brother is under a lot of stress."

"Yeah," Barry chimed in. "Being a legendary hero isn't like coming up to bat in a baseball game in the bottom of the ninth with the bases loaded and the game on the line. There is no tomorrow. If you strike out in this game, people die."

"Baseball? Strike out?" said Adon in a perplexed tone. "I do not understand those words. The responsibilities of the Turok lineage are clear. Turok must meet all threats to the safety and security of Earth. What is there to think about? I accept my duty to speak for the Council of Voices. Turoks are born to defend Earth and Galyanna."

Alison and Barry glared at Adon. Sometimes she seemed more like a

141

computer program than a person, which in a sense she was. She didn't comprehend or understand human feelings like guilt, depression, or remorse. To her there was just right, wrong, and responsibility.

"Forget it, guys," Josh said to Alison and Barry. "Adon isn't like we are. She can't feel the things we do." He looked at Adon. "Tell me about the Campaigner's Arena," he asked changing the subject. "What is he like? What can I expect when we reach his arena?"

As Adon began to speak, her eyes stared into Josh's eyes. "Expect trouble," Adon advised. "The Campaigner is Galyanna's most notorious and powerful warlord. He shows no mercy to his foes and he expects none in return. In the Campaigner's Arena, there is only one rule: kill or be killed! So you must be careful not to . . . to . . . strike out, as you put it."

Barry gulped. He glanced at Alison. "This Campaigner dude sounds like an ancient Roman emperor presiding over battles between gladiators." He shuddered. "Do we have to go to his arena?"

"We do if we want to secure the Energy Totem that is held within the arena complex," Adon answered.

"Can't we reason with him?" Alison asked.

Adon slowly shook her head. "Combat is the only reasoning that the Campaigner can understand," Adon replied. "He is a huge, brutish being who has a particular dislike for Turoks." She looked at Joshua. "In order to secure the Energy Totem for safekeeping you will doubtless have to battle against his stable of warrior champions."

Joshua looked at Adon. "Wonderful," Josh grumbled. "In order to keep from fighting Primagen's marauding hordes for possession of the Energy Totem, all I have to do is match myself in hand-to-hand combat against the Campaigner's bloodthirsty gladiators."

"Welcome to Galyanna, the friendly Lost Land that delights in dismembering its visitors and tourists," Barry remarked to Josh sarcastically.

Alison hit him in the ribs with her elbow. "That's not funny," she scolded. "What chance will Josh possibly have against the Campaigner's skilled, well-trained killers?"

"Thanks for the confidence, Ali," replied Josh.

Adon looked at her companions. "The Campaigner does have one redeeming quality," she stated. "He never goes back on his word. If you can get him to

143

promise you something, he will always live up to that promise." She paused to look directly at Joshua. "However, be careful what you agree to. He will take advantage of you if at all possible."

Josh rolled his eyes. "Oh that sounds encouraging," he said. "All I have to do is convince a bloodthirsty maniac who never breaks his word to give up his Energy Totem. It sounds like a piece of cake."

Barry shook his head. "I don't think I understand," he muttered. "Fighting to the death? Why? What purpose can such senseless brutality accomplish, even in Galyanna?"

"The Campaigner believes that continual mortal combat in his arena weeds out the weak species in The Lost Land. He feels he is providing a much-needed service to the ultimate evolution of Galyanna."

Looking over the edge of the hovercraft Joshua saw the myriad of burning craters below. "Maybe the Campaigner needs a lesson in compassion," he said. "Survival of the fittest doesn't always mean the cruelest warrior is the best choice to stay alive. Physical strength doesn't always exceed the power of the mind or the heart."

"Look who's turned into a philosopher,"

said Barry. "Socrates, Plato, and now Fireseed."

"Hey, that's Turok to you, pal," Alison reminded Barry.

"What if I refuse to fight?" asked Josh.

"In the Campaigner's Arena," began Adon, "if you want to live to see another day, then you not only fight, but you must kill those who oppose you."

Josh nodded solemnly. "We'll see about that," he said. The hovercraft continued on toward the arena of the cruel, war-loving Campaigner.

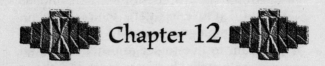

# Chapter 12

The hovercraft touched down in a barren field of volcanic rock and shallow pools of bubbling brown muck. Large pockets of air and mud exploded as they rose to the surface, releasing bursts of foul-smelling gasses.

"What a revolting place," Alison grunted in disgust. "Galyanna may be the sewer of the universe, but this part is definitely the armpit of The Lost Land."

"And it sure could use a powerful deodorant," added Barry as he clamped two fingers over his nose.

Josh ignored their remarks and stepped out of the hovercraft. Approximately a hundred yards from where they'd landed stood a huge, circular structure made out of large slabs of stone.

The arena was three stories high and as big around as a football stadium back on Earth. There was a single arch that served as an entrance. The arch was sealed shut by two enormous wooden doors. "Well, what do we do now?" Josh asked Adon.

"We wait," she replied calmly.

"Wait?" gagged Alison as she choked on the gassy fumes. "For what?"

"For the Pur-linn to arrive," the Speaker of Forever Light said. "They are the brutish, apelike allies of the Campaigner. They serve him as guards and soldiers."

Josh, Barry, and Alison turned as the huge wooden doors of the arena swung open with a loud bang. Out of the arena marched a troop of ugly creatures dressed in dull armor, carrying a wide array of primitive weapons ranging from pointy lances and huge battle-axes to large, razor-sharp swords and gleaming cleavers. The troop consisted of seventeen Pur-linn soldiers. One particularly large soldier led the group while the others trudged along behind him in two sloppy columns.

As the Pur-linn warriors got closer,

Alison leaned over and whispered to Josh. "They look like that ape-thing you battled at the apple tree," she said. Josh nodded.

"I fought a creature like these near the fruit-gatherers' village," he told Adon. "But it didn't wear armor or carry a weapon."

"That was a War Club," Adon explained. "War Clubs are a more primitive class of Pur-linn."

The Pur-linn headsman halted his troop in front of the hovercraft. He shouldered his giant gleaming cleaver and stared suspiciously at Adon.

"Turok and I seek an immediate audience with your master, the Campaigner," Adon told the headsman.

The headsman visibly reacted when he heard the name. *Turok*. His brow wrinkled as he studied Joshua, looking him over from head to toe. The creature's lips curled up in a hideous twisted smirk and it let out a sickly, bellowing grunt of a laugh. It lifted its cleaver and pointed at the great wooden gates leading into the arena.

"I guess that's an invitation," Josh said. Adon stepped off the hovercraft and joined Joshua.

"I'm ready," Barry called out. "Let's go."

Adon quickly spun to face Alison and

Barry. She held up her hand ordering them to halt. "It is best if you remain at the hovercraft," she advised. "The Campaigner considers all visitors to his realm as possible combatants for his arena. *Fodder*, as he calls them." She stared at Barry.

He gulped. "Are you saying that the Campaigner would view us as weak individuals he'd like to . . . as you put it before . . . weed out?"

"Weak?" grunted Alison. "Weed out? I'll kick that egotistical brute right in his Lost Land butt!" She stormed off the craft. Barry followed.

"NO!" Josh yelled. He stopped his sister. "Adon is right. It's better if you and Barry stay here. Why put yourself in danger? It's bad enough that I have to deal with this bloodthirsty maniac. If I have to fight for the totem, which I hope I don't, I don't want to be worrying about whether you and Barry are safe."

"But if you have to fight, I want to be there," Alison insisted stubbornly.

Barry touched Alison's shoulder. "We can best help Josh by staying here," he said. "We'll just wait in the car, Josh," he added, pointing to the hovercraft.

Alison gave Barry the evil eye.

Barry returned her stare. "I'm not saying this because I'm afraid of what might happen to us in there." He pointed a finger in the direction of the arena. "I'm thinking about what's best for Josh. If he has to worry about us, it will be harder for him to get the totem from this clown. Look, before you know it, we'll all be back in the hovercraft, heading for the nearest Lost Land pizza joint."

Alison inhaled a deep breath and exhaled loudly. She bit her lower lip and tapped her foot impatiently. "Okay! Okay!" she said, finally giving in. "I'll stay here . . . for now." She stepped back in the hovercraft. Barry did likewise.

The Pur-linn headsman grunted. He motioned toward the arena again. The Pur-linn troopers lined up behind Adon and Joshua. The headsman lumbered off toward his evil master's headquarters.

"Do not forget that the Campaigner is a master of trickery, young Turok," Adon advised Josh. "He hates all Turoks. Many have beaten previous Campaigners in the past. He would like nothing better than to see your blood stain the ground of his arena."

Josh nodded. He swallowed hard. There was a lump in his throat. He wasn't a coward—he'd already proven that to everyone—including himself. Nevertheless, he was a bit afraid. He didn't know what to expect. "There have been other Campaigners?" he asked Adon.

"Many," she replied. "When one is killed in the arena, the next in line takes his place."

The Pur-linn headsman halted at the ten-foot-high wooden doors that barred their entrance into the Campaigner's Arena. The creature reached up and clasped a thick metal ring in his big, hairy hand. Then the headsman banged the ring against the door three times.

*BOOM! BOOM! BOOM!* The sound echoed through the arena. Slowly, the massive doors both opened to reveal the bowels of the great stone structure.

To Josh's shock and alarm, he instantly became a witness to a savage battle coming to a brutal and bloody conclusion in the center of the arena.

A creature that he now knew to be a War Club was sprawled on the ground at the feet of a Dinosoid warrior. The War Club was bleeding profusely from an open socket where an arm had once been. The severed limb was lying on the ground.

The Dinosoid warrior raised a curved sword above his head and then plunged its tip into the chest of the helpless War Club. The loser of the battle died instantly.

The Pur-linn troopers rushed out and proclaimed the Dinosoid the victor. Other Pur-linns collected the body of the loser and quickly dragged it out of sight.

Josh shook his head in disgust. The sight sickened him to his stomach. He lowered his head to look at the ground. The Pur-linn headsman grunted. Josh looked up. The ape-like brute motioned for Josh to move forward.

"No!" Adon refused. She reached out with her arm and prevented Josh from entering the structure. "Anyone who enters the arena of their own free will is fair game for combat," she stated. "It is the Campaigner's rule. And it is a rule he never fails to exploit." Adon looked at the headsman. "Bring your master to us. We will wait here."

The headsman nodded. He led his troops into the arena, while Josh and Adon waited at the open gates. Minutes later, a monstrous green and red hulk appeared in the doorway. Its face was ravaged and hideous. Its huge, muscular body was grossly deformed. Its feet had three large toes. At the end of each toe was a thick sharp talon. The brute's torso was as wide as a tree trunk, and it had huge arms and hands. Protruding out of its back were rows of thick pointed humps. The grotesque monster put its hands on its hips and rocked its head back and forth as it gazed upon the visitors.

"The Campaigner welcomes the Speaker of Forever Light," he greeted. There was more than a hint of contempt in his voice. "So this is the new Turok! He's a mere child!" The Campaigner roared in laughter. When he stopped, he took two steps forward and scrutinized Josh more closely. "Have you come to fight?" he inquired hopefully.

"No," Josh answered boldly. "I have no reason to fight."

The Campaigner was taken aback by Josh's response. "Here we fight to live and live to fight! That is reason enough!" he roared.

"I don't want to fight," Josh said sternly.

"Then why have you come here?" the Campaigner demanded.

"I've come to collect the Energy Totem you have in your arena," Josh explained.

"Ahh, yes, the Energy Totem," the Campaigner said, as if he understood everything. "It is moored to the balcony next to my own throne. Primagen needs it and you want it. But it is the Campaigner who has it."

"If Galyanna is destroyed," Adon said softly, "we will all perish."

"Death is but a part of life," the Campaigner said, shrugging off her warning. "In the arena we understand and appreciate the beauty of dying well." He looked at Josh. "Are you prepared to die well, Turok? Will you risk your life to save Galyanna?"

"I'll do what I have to do," Josh replied sternly. "But I won't kill just to appease your twisted sense of competition."

Once again the Campaigner roared in laughter. "The acid of your words has burned into my brain, Turok. I hear and understand. You will not kill."

"I will not," Josh adamantly stated. "Now will you give us the Energy Totem for safe-keeping?"

"I will on one condition," the Campaigner said. "Four times in the past, Campaigners have been defeated by other Turoks in combat. If you agree to fight four opponents of my choosing and you defeat them, I will give you the Energy Totem."

Josh put his hand on his chin and stroked it thoughtfully. There seemed to be no other way to proceed. Taking the totem by force was out of the question. The arena was too heavily guarded.

"Do you give me your word that if I defeat my foes I can take the totem?" he said slyly. He remembered what Adon had told him about the Campaigner's unflinching sense of honor.

"I do . . . if you'll give me your word to follow my rules of combat," the Campaigner replied. "You need not even answer. Just walk into the arena if the bargain is agreeable to you."

Driven by a sense of bravado, Joshua Fireseed strolled courageously out into the center of the bloodstained arena before Adon could stop him.

"Fool," mocked the Campaigner. "You say you will not kill but you've agreed to abide by my rules of combat. My rules are simple. Fight to live. To live is to win. To lose is to die. To win the totem you must kill your opponents." The Campaigner howled in laughter. "The Energy Totem shall be yours only when your opponents lie bloody and lifeless at your feet."

Joshua looked at Adon for help. She shook her head. She could do nothing to assist him.

155

"A bargain has been made, Turok," she said. "You must follow the rules."

Josh's face hardened. Every muscle in his body tensed. He'd been too quick to agree to the Campaigner's terms. He'd been tricked. But Joshua Fireseed was nobody's fool. The only rules he played by were his own.

"Bring on my first opponent," he called to the Campaigner. The Campaigner ordered the doors of the arena shut and barred. He ascended to his stone throne high above the arena floor. Next to the throne stood the Energy Totem, pulsating with power.

"Send in the Flesh Eater Sentinel called Ripscar," the Campaigner ordered. A Purlinn trooper standing near a wooden doorway directly across from the Campaigner's throne nodded. The trooper opened the door and a repulsive sentinel of Galyanna's most dreaded military cult entered the arena.

The Flesh Eaters were a grisly, terrifying race who lived in a remote mountain stronghold. They were fierce, fearless fighters who delighted in ripping apart and eating the flesh of their opponents.

Ripscar was big. He towered over Turok. On his body he wore magnificent armor that protected his massive arms, legs and torso. He was armed with two huge curved blades that ran the length of his lower arms and extended two feet out beyond the reach of his hands.

"Hand-to-hand combat is the rule, Turok," the Campaigner called. "Arm yourself." The Campaigner waved his hand. The Flesh Eater Sentinel began to lumber forward.

"It looks like Ripscar is a blade man," Josh said. "Against him, I'll need a weapon that can really cut the mustard." He stuck his right hand deep into the Light Burden. Josh withdrew his hand from the satchel and produced a Saquin talon. The sharp twin-bladed weapon was strapped to his hand with thick strips of leather. In the hands of a skilled Saquin warrior it was definitely a deadly weapon.

The Sentinel crouched low as he faced Turok. He swung his right arm in a circular motion in an attempt to slice the young warrior in half. Josh leaped back and avoided the slashing maneuver. The two combatants carefully circled each other looking for an opening.

The Sentinel lunged forward. Ripscar cut downward in a chopping motion. The Flesh Eater's blade came so close that a few strands of Turok's thick black hair were sheared off.

"A close shave, but no prize," Turok mocked.

The enraged Sentinel attacked Turok with increased ferocity. It whirled its arms, churning its forearm blades like spinning buzzsaws. Turok used his talon to block savage slash after slash. Steel clashed against steel as thrust after thrust was harmlessly deflected by the young Saquin warrior.

"If you can't beat 'em, wear 'em down," Josh said as he skillfully evaded another swipe at his mid-section. *I'm not sure if my breastplate will protect me from that blade,* he thought as he moved his body out of the way. *But I sure don't want to find out the hard way!*

Slowly but surely the Flesh Eater Sentinel began to tire. Never before had an opponent managed to dodge blow after blow. Ripscar whirled to face his agile foe. He lashed out again with his blade. The point missed Turok and stuck in the ground of the arena. Turok saw his chance. He cartwheeled behind the sentinel and sprang up onto his back. He locked his knees on Ripscar's back and wrapped his free arm around the Flesh Eater's neck in a stronghold. Placing the razor-sharp talon near the sentinel's neck, he yelled, "Yield or die!"

Ripscar fell to his knees. "I . . . yield," he

rasped as he collapsed and fell face first into the dirt.

"Kill him!" shouted the Campaigner from his throne. "Kill him!"

"No!" Turok refused. "The match is over. I win!"

The Campaigner waved his fist angrily in the air. According to their bargain, he could have ordered his guards to execute Turok for not holding up his end of the agreement. But he much preferred to see the young warrior fight and die on the battlefield of his arena. "The next time you won't be so lucky," he vowed. "Bring out Goliath!"

Almost at once another door in the bottom level of the arena slid open. A dark, hunched-over form emerged from the doorway. Once out in the arena, the thing stood up to its full height. Goliath was a giant Purlinn mutant who stood twelve feet tall. The beast carried a spiked club that had been chiseled out of the trunk of a great tree. As soon as Goliath laid eyes on Turok, it charged. Luckily for Turok the great lumbering beast was slow-footed.

"If you're Goliath, I guess that makes me David," Josh quipped. He stuck both hands into the Light Burden. With his right hand he retracted an ancient

159

sling. In his left he pulled out a strangely-shaped rock and returned the Saguin talon to its place in the mystical Turok arsenal.

"Here goes nothing," Turok said. He fitted the odd rock in the sling and whirled it above his head. Step by thunderous step, Goliath, the giant Pur-linn mutant was bearing down on him. Turok released the rock. The stony missile sped through the air and struck Goliath in the middle of the forehead right between the eyes.

*BLAM!* The oddly-shaped rock exploded, surprising even Josh. It was a concussion stone. The blast stopped Goliath in mid-stride. The giant was reeling. It dropped its weapon and clutched its aching head. It spun on its bare heels and then toppled like a felled tree. Goliath crashed to the floor of the arena.

"Finish him!" the Campaigner hollered. "This time follow the rules. Finish him! Goliath must die!"

"No, " refused Joshua Fireseed. "The battle is over. Once again I win. But I won't kill a helpless foe." He turned his back on the fallen giant and walked to the center of the arena.

Outside of the arena, Alison and Barry were beginning to worry. Josh and Adon had been gone a long time. When Alison spied

Adon returning to the hovercraft alone, she couldn't contain herself.

"Where's Josh?" she demanded.

"Turok is fighting in the arena," Adon replied calmly. "If he wins, the Campaigner will give us the energy totem."

"And what if he loses?" Alison asked.

"If he loses he will die," Adon stated matter-of-factly. "But do not concern yourself with such troubling thoughts. He is a Turok! He will win."

"Right," replied Alison angrily. "All Turoks are invincible. Just ask my Uncle Carl." Alison ran toward the arena.

"Your presence at the arena will only hinder your brother's chances for ultimate victory," Adon called out.

"Wait, Alison!" Barry shouted. "I'm going with you." Barry raced off after Alison. Together they bolted away from the hovercraft. In a matter of minutes the two frenzied friends reached the gates of the arena. The great wooden doors were closed tight.

Alison pounded on the doors with her fists. "Let us in," she demanded.

Barry turned around. He gulped. "Y-You can stop pounding, Alison," Barry sputtered. "I think they heard us." Alison stopped. She turned around.

161

The Pur-linn headsman and four Pur-linn troopers were standing behind them. The troopers lowered their spears. "Uh-oh," Barry lamented. "I don't suppose these guys are ushers, here to show us to our seats in the stands. I think we're in big trouble."

At that same moment Joshua Fireseed was squaring off against his third opponent in the arena. Once again the Campaigner was counting on a combatant to finish off Turok, providing him with more entertainment than a simple execution would.

Turok's foe was a lean, yellow-skinned alien gladiator with a serpentine head. The gladiator had a human body and was armed with a shield and a phaser trident. The three-pronged trident was not only pointed and sharp, but also delivered a numbing shock whenever it came in contact with an opponent. Turok now was defending himself with a jewel-handled combat knife.

"You must die, Turok, you coward," the gladiator hissed. His long split tongue shot out between his gleaming curved fangs. "I have killed many opponents in the arena and you will be my next victim." The gladiator faked an attack to the left and lunged to the right. The phaser trident nicked Turok's left arm.

*FIZZZT!* The shock caused Josh to yell in pain. *"ARRRRAUGH!"* he cried as his entire arm went numb. The useless limb dropped limply to his side. It hung there as the life-and-death contest continued.

"Now I have you," the gladiator hissed. The alien's snake tongue whipped in and out of his mouth. Its viper eyes twinkled as it closed in for the kill. "Die, Turok!" the gladiator cried. It thrust the trident at Turok's chest. The points struck the Saquin's mystical protective breastplate. A spark of energy filled the air. The charge was negated and the trident's sharp edges never so much as scratched Turok's flesh. In a flash Turok whirled. With a mighty chop of his combat knife he cut the phaser trident in two.

"No," gasped the gladiator who was now, unarmed except for his shield. Turok dropped his knife. With his left arm hanging limply at his side he curled his right hand into a fist. Instantly he cocked his good arm, made a fist, and delivered a crushing blow to the snout of the alien viper. The punch landed with such force that the gladiator's head rocked back. Turok cocked his fist and punched again. The second punch caused the snake's eyes to roll

163

back in its head. It fell to the ground dazed and helpless.

Quickly, Turok picked up his combat knife. His left arm tingled as feeling slowly returned to it. With knife in hand he stood over his fallen foe.

"Cut his throat!" the Campaigner raged. "I order you to kill him. Follow the rules of my arena. Kill or be killed!" He jumped to his feet. "Kill! Kill to live! Live to kill! Stab him!"

Joshua Fireseed slowly shook his head. He reached back and threw his knife at the arena wall beneath the Campaigner's throne. *THUNK!* The blade sank deep into the wall and stuck. "This contest is over!" Josh declared. "I win. Now keep your word and give me the Energy Totem."

In a furious rage the Campaigner leaped down from his throne ledge and landed on the floor of the arena. He glared at the young Turok. "The contest is not yet over," he announced. "You have one more opponent to face. And this time you will die!"

Turok faced the hideous monstrosity before him. "Who is my last opponent?" he demanded to know.

"I am," the Campaigner declared as he thumped his chest with his hand. "And if I do not kill you, which I plan to do, you will have to kill me to win. It is the rule."

Joshua Fireseed grinned. "Don't you know by now that I refuse to play by your rules, Campaigner?"

"This time," promised the Campaigner, "you will obey my rules or suffer the dire consequences—to yourself and to them!" He waved his hand.

A trap door in the side of the arena opened. Barry and Alison were forced out of the doorway by the Campaigner's guards. Their hands were securely tied behind their backs. The two most important people in Joshua Fireseed's life at that moment stumbled forward.

"If I win and kill you, they die, too," the Campaigner stated. "If you win and do not obey the rules and kill me, your companions will be instantly executed. Your one hope for your friends' survival is to kill me." The Campaigner roared in laughter. "Now whose rules are we playing by, Turok?"

Josh glanced at his sister and his best friend, who were being dragged to the center of the arena by the Campaigner's guards. They were both helpless pawns in the Campaigner's insane test of physical prowess and combat skills. Josh took a deep breath. He had sworn to protect Alison and Barry at all costs. What choice did he have now except to fight to the death?

The Campaigner raised his powerful arm. "Let the battle begin!" he shouted.

# The TUROK Adventures!

#1 *Way of the Warrior*
#2 *Seeds of Evil*
#3 *Arena of Doom*
(in stores December 1998)
#4 *Path of Destruction*
(in stores January 1999)